THE VIBRATIONS OF LOVE

Fabia's hands were clasped together, her head was bent, and the Duke was aware that she was praying. The Duke rose and walked towards her.

"I . . . I had to come," she said. "I . . . I was . . . afraid."

"There is no need to be," he said. Very gently the Duke put his arms around her. "Your prayers have been answered."

She looked up at him. "You mean . . . ?"

"I mean," he said gently, "the only woman I want in my life is you, and I know now that I cannot live without you."

Then his lips were on hers. At first he kissed her gently, tenderly, and for the moment without passion, because everything that had happened made him feel as if they were part of something sacred and divine. Then his arms tightened, and his lips became more demanding, insistent. . . .

Bantam Books by Barbara Cartland
Ask your bookseller for the books you have missed

About Barbara Cartland
CRUSADER IN PINK

The Vibrations of Love

Barbara Cartland

BANTAM BOOKS
TORONTO · NEW YORK · LONDON · SYDNEY

THE VIBRATIONS OF LOVE
A Bantam Book / March 1982

ISBN 0-553-20746-6

Published simultaneously in the United States and Canada

Bantam Books are published by Bantam Books, Inc. Its trade-
mark, consisting of the words "Bantam Books" and the por-
trayal of a rooster, is Registered in U.S. Patent and Trademark
Office and in other countries. Marca Registrada. Bantam
Books, Inc., 666 Fifth Avenue, New York, New York 10103.

PRINTED IN THE UNITED STATES OF AMERICA

0 9 8 7 6 5 4 3 2 1

Author's Note

My mother, before she died at age ninety-eight, was thrilled with television.

"How could I ever imagine," she asked, "that I could lie in bed and watch the races I attended as a girl?"

In the '20s I was equally thrilled with the first wireless I listened to and spoke on. But the "Magic Mirror on the Wall" was part of our fairy-stories, and the power and force of vibrations have been known to primitive people since the beginning of time.

I remember once when I was motoring in the dark, screaming as the car I was in ran into a flock of sheep. In the headlights I could see the terror in the animals' eyes as they struggled to get away. Then I was suddenly aware that it was "just my imagination."

When we stopped a little way on at a Country Inn, I was told that the accident I had just seen had taken place five years earlier.

That was a case of a photograph on the atmosphere and accounts for many of the murders and other crimes of violence that people "see" in ancient buildings.

The
Vibrations
of Love

Chapter One

1842

The Lord Chamberlain appeared nervous as the Duke watched him fiddling with the blotter on his desk, straightening the ink-pot, and moving a letter-opener.

Finally the Lord Chamberlain said:

"I think, Your Grace, you must have some idea of what I am about to say to you."

"Not the slightest!" the Duke replied.

He was sitting back comfortably in the chair in front of the desk with his legs crossed and appeared completely at his ease.

The Lord Chamberlain glanced at him and thought the Duke was in fact one of the best-looking men he had ever seen and it was not surprising that his reputation with women was so infamous that it had come to Her Majesty's attention.

However, as the Duke always behaved with the utmost propriety at Buckingham Palace and Windsor Castle, there had been nothing the Queen could say or do.

And yet, undoubtedly because no-one whether living in a cottage or a Royal Palace could prevent women from talking, the gossip about the Duke had increased year after year until at last it had assumed such proportions that trouble was unavoidable.

It was true that Her Majesty had perhaps allowed the Duke more licence than was usual because she liked handsome men, and in some ways the Duke bore a vague resemblance to her beloved Albert.

But if that was true of their physical appearance, in every other particular the two men were the antithesis of each other.

The Prince, stiff, conscientious, solemn, determined that protocol should be observed on all occasions, was very different from the third Duke of Ilminster.

Ever since leaving Eton the Duke had enjoyed life to the full, moving from one scandal to another, all invariably involving beautiful women, with a bewildering rapidity.

On the race-course he was a sportsman beloved by the crowds and would no more have swerved from the strictest rules of the Turf than he would have cheated at cards.

But where women were concerned the rules of sportsmanship did not apply, and husbands ground their teeth with fury when the Duke entered a Ball-Room, and mothers hurried their daughters away with the protective instinct of a hen confronted by a fox.

Needless to say, the Duke was not in the least interested in girls, but only in the attractive, sophisticated, witty Society beauties who amused him for a short time before his interest was aroused by a new face or the curves of a new figure.

But now, as was inevitable, nemesis had caught up with him, and it was the Lord Chamberlain's unpleasant duty to convey Her Majesty's disapproval to a man whom secretly in his heart he envied.

"Suppose you tell me frankly," the Duke said as the Lord Chamberlain still hesitated, "what is in your mind?"

"Not my mind, Ilminster," the Lord Chamberlain replied, "but Her Majesty's."

"I might have guessed that," the Duke said with a slightly cynical smile.

Despite his handsome looks there had in the last year or two appeared on his face the lines of a man who had often been disillusioned and who no longer approached life with the same carefree excitement as he had felt when he was younger.

In fact, the Duke was more often bored than amused, and the reason his *affaires de coeur* lasted such a short time and changed so frequently was that he found that women inevitably said the same and were the same once the excitement of the chase was over.

"Ilminster has broken more hearts than I have votes," one Member of Parliament said jokingly in the House of Commons, while the Betting-book at White's regularly recorded large amounts of money wagered on how long the Duke's latest favourite would last.

The Lord Chamberlain cleared his throat.

"Her Majesty has unfortunately been informed of what happened in the Picture-Gallery the evening before last."

"I am naturally willing to replace the vase that was broken," the Duke said.

"That is what she expected you would do," the Lord Chamberlain replied, "but it is not that it was broken which has upset the Queen, but the cause of the damage occurring in the first place."

The Duke thought he might have anticipated that was the attitude Her Majesty and the Prince Consort would take, and, as the Lord Chamberlain had said, it was certainly unfortunate.

He had been walking down the Gallery, being on duty as Lord-in-Waiting, when he had seen coming towards him one of Her Majesty's younger and prettier Ladies-in-Waiting.

She was a flirtatious little piece whom he had noticed eying him invitingly on several occasions, but he had paid no attention to her because at the time he had been otherwise pleasantly engaged.

Now she stopped to talk to him, and it was impossible not to be aware that she was eagerly and excitedly expecting him to do something outrageous. So what could he do but oblige?

He had swept her into his arms and she had returned his kisses in a manner which told him all too clearly that she had been frustrated in having to wait so long for them.

Only when he became more passionate and demanding did she make a little protest and struggle, not very determinedly but enough to excite him further.

The Duke then made a suggestion at which she pretended to be shocked, and when she struggled again he let her go quite suddenly. This was so unexpected to her that she staggered and half-fell against a large Chinese vase that stood somewhat insecurely on a carved ebony stand beside them.

The Duke put out his hand to save it, but it was too late.

She knocked the vase with her elbow and it crashed onto the polished floor, breaking into a dozen pieces.

They both stared down at the damage in dismay, and with a little cry of sheer terror the Lady-in-Waiting picked up the front of her gown and ran as quickly as she could down the passage and out of sight.

Unfortunately, as she did so she was seen and so was the Duke, together with the broken vase, by one of the Prince Consort's toadies who felt it his duty to convey to his Royal Highness news of anything which happened, assuming that in doing so he added to his own importance.

He came fussily up to the Duke, who was still contemplating the broken pieces of china at his feet, to say:

"You have broken a valuable vase, Your Grace!"

"That is obvious," the Duke replied blandly.

"Her Majesty will be extremely annoyed, since His Royal Highness has only just finished arranging the furniture in this Gallery."

"Then His Royal Highness will have to find another vase," the Duke had remarked, and then had walked away before he had to listen to any more.

He thought now that it must have given the officious, pompous gentleman in question great pleasure to write a report of what had occurred.

He only felt sorry for the Lady-in-Waiting, who would, if nothing worse, be severely reprimanded for her part in the incident, and if she had not been seen he would have been quite prepared to take on himself full blame for the accident.

"Well, how am I supposed to show my contrition?" he asked now. "Stand in a corner?"

"I am afraid that is what it amounts to," the Lord Chamberlain replied. "Her Majesty suggests that you will enjoy being in the country for the next two months, rather than pursue your arduous duties in the Palace."

The Duke threw back his head and laughed.

"You are quite right, My Lord," he said. "I am to stand in the corner! I am only surprised that you are not expected also to give me six of the best!"

The Lord Chamberlain smiled a little ruefully.

"I have not particularly enjoyed my task of having to tell you this, Your Grace," he said, "but I rather expected it to happen sooner or later."

"Do not worry," the Duke replied, "and let me tell you—and it is not a matter of sour grapes—that I have begun to think lately that the ceremonial of the Palace is a dead bore."

"We all feel that at times," the Lord Chamberlain answered with a sigh.

"It makes me think I was born in the wrong reign," the Duke said. "I would have enjoyed myself far more if Her Majesty's uncle were still on the throne."

The Lord Chamberlain knew that he was referring to George IV, whose outrageous behaviour as Regent with his extravagances and his plump mistresses had made the parties at Carlton House the best entertainment in London.

Buckingham Palace also, which owed its impressive elegance entirely to him, had been a joy to visit and a delight in which to work.

When he thought about it, the Lord Chamberlain knew that the Duke was right and that environment would have suited him perfectly.

His behaviour was in fact very Georgian, and his worst excesses would hardly have caused the raising of an eye-brow in the reign of "The Prince of Pleasure," when no-one was concerned with anything except amusing themselves.

In contrast, the earnest desire of the Prince Consort and his adoring wife, Victoria, "to be good" certainly made the Assemblies at Buckingham Palace more like psalm-singing religious meetings than enjoyable Royal evenings.

The Duke recalled the Lord Chamberlain from his contemplation of the difference between George IV and his niece by asking:

"Is that all?"

"I should have thought it was quite enough," the Lord Chamberlain replied. "I can only say again, Your Grace, that I am sorry I had to be the conveyor of bad news."

"Do not worry," the Duke said. "I do not bemoan my fate, nor will it worry me particularly not to be in the Royal Box at Ascot. I shall have my own, and I hope you will join me for a drink when my horse wins the Gold Cup."

The Lord Chamberlain laughed and rose to his feet.

"You are very confident of your success."

"Why not?" the Duke asked. "I have the best horse!"

When he had left the room, the Lord Chamberlain added to himself:

"And the best of everything else!"

* * *

The Duke awoke the next morning with a heavy head and dry mouth and the conviction that he had been extremely foolish in celebrating his disgrace in an excessive indulgence, which was uncharacteristic of him.

Although his parties were often outrageous and sometimes exceedingly drunken, he himself was on the whole abstemious.

Yesterday, after he had left the Lord Chamberlain's office, he had invited a number of his closest friends to dine with him at his house in Park Lane.

After a superlative dinner during which the toasts had been too frequent, they had gone on to one of Lady Duncan's parties, which were notorious for being outrageous but which the Duke found exceedingly amusing.

Lady Duncan had been an actress—although by professional standards that was rather a flattering word for it—who had inveigled an elderly and in fact senile Peer into marrying her.

Although he was exceedingly rich, she made no attempt to enter Society, which had anyway closed their doors to her. Instead, at her house in Grosvenor Square she entertained beautiful women who in their turn attracted gentlemen who appreciated Molly Duncan's hospitality, which in its way was unique.

The women who graced Lady Duncan's parties were drawn at first entirely from the stage or from an older and more disreputable profession.

Then gradually a number of those on the fringe of Society, or those who although well born had been ostracised by the more particular hostesses, also accepted invitations to Duncan House.

Lady Duncan's guests had gradually become a mixture of all types and classes, although at the same time everyone there came under one label of being entertaining.

Men who were at a loose end or who found themselves with nowhere particular to go after a good dinner made their way to Duncan House on the three evenings a week that "Queen Molly" was at home.

Last night, when the Duke had appeared with his friends, she had flung up her arms with a cry of delight and run down the stairs to kiss him passionately.

She was still a very pretty woman with a full figure, eyes that sparkled like champagne, and hair that glittered like a gold crown.

What also glittered was the wealth of diamonds which encircled her long white neck, hung from her ears, and weighed down her slender wrists.

"I have missed you!" she complained to the Duke. "How could you neglect me for so long?"

"It is a dull story," the Duke replied, "and now that I am back, do not bore me with recriminations."

"I have never bored you yet," Molly Duncan replied, "and your friends will not be bored either. Some very pretty women have just arrived from Paris."

The Frenchwomen had certainly been gay and very attractive, the Duke remembered.

But instead of concentrating on them, he had made the mistake of allowing himself to be monopolised by Dilys Chertsey.

Lady Dilys Chertsey was another who had incurred the Queen's displeasure and was definitely on the "Black List" at Buckingham Palace.

The daughter of a Duke, when she was still at School she had run away with a handsome Army Officer whom she had found irresistible in his uniform and a bore when he took it off.

Fortunately for his wife, he had been killed in a shooting accident after they had been married for only three years.

Dilys had not returned to her family but instead had set up house on her own and proceeded to enjoy herself in a way that the great hostesses considered extremely improper.

However, it was difficult for them to ignore her

completely, considering the social importance of her father and mother, the Duke being very much *persona grata* with the Queen.

The hostesses did their best to avoid Dilys, who made no overtures to them anyway, but they talked about her incessantly in lowered voices.

In the meantime, Dilys, extremely beautiful and with enough money not to need the support of anybody in her wild life, began to enjoy herself.

The Duke was well aware that she had been pursuing him for some time, but because he thought it would be a mistake to be embroiled with somebody who was almost as notorious as he was, he had in fact deliberately avoided her.

At the same time, it was impossible not to admire Dilys for her beauty and her expertise.

Because last night he had been celebrating his disgrace a little too freely, he had succumbed to her blandishments and at dawn he had removed himself with difficulty from her bed and begun to put on his clothes preparatory to returning home.

He remembered now in retrospect that she had looked exceedingly alluring with her flaming red hair flowing over the pillows, her green eyes glinting at him from under dark lashes.

Then as he recalled the scene he remembered that as he had walked towards the door, his feet feeling as crooked as his tie, she had said:

"Good-bye, Vian. You have made me very happy, and when you are feeling less tired we will arrange our plans . . ."

The Duke was almost through the door by this time, and now incredibly, terrifyingly, he was almost certain that the last three words he had heard when he was out in the passage were: "to be married."

'I could not have heard that,' he suddenly thought. 'I must have been dreaming!'

But now that his brain was clearer and the effect of

what he had drunk had worn off after a few hours' sleep, he was almost prepared to swear that that was what she had said.

"It is impossible!" he murmured, and rang for his Valet.

*   *   *

An hour later the Duke was downstairs making a pretence at eating breakfast when the door opened and the Butler announced:

"Major Edward Bicester, Your Grace!"

The Duke pushed aside his plate, from which he had eaten nothing, and looked up with relief as his closest friend and confidant came into the room.

"Good-morning, Vian," he said as he approached the table. "How can you be up so early after such a hell of a night?"

"I had to see you, Eddie," the Duke replied.

Major Bicester lowered himself somewhat carefully into a chair which the Butler held for him, and when asked what he would have he merely replied:

"Brandy, and plenty of it!"

With an impassive face the Butler put a glass beside him, poured out a liberal helping of brandy with a small amount of soda, and left both the decanter and the syphon on the table.

Then, following his master's regular instructions, he withdrew from the Breakfast-Room and closed the door behind him.

Edward Bicester drank some of the brandy before he said:

"You look disgustingly well after such a hectic night."

"I do not feel it!" the Duke murmured.

"Nor do I," Eddie answered. "If you ask me, Molly's wine deteriorates as the evening progresses. It is an old trick and one we should be prepared for by now. I am quite certain that what one is offered towards the end of the party is not the same quality that one drinks at the beginning."

"That happens in a great many houses," the Duke remarked. "But I did not invite you here this morning to discuss Molly's hospitality, or rather, not directly."

Eddie looked at him apprehensively.

"What has happened?" he asked.

"I drank too much last night."

"I thought you did," Eddie agreed, "and it is unlike you, Vian. You are usually so abstemious. But of course you had an excuse for your excesses."

"A damned silly one," the Duke said, "and after all, it was only an excuse for a party."

"I do not think I have ever had a better dinner there," Eddie said reflectively.

"I do not want to talk about the dinner," the Duke replied, "but what happened afterwards."

Eddie took another drink.

"What did happen?" he asked.

"Because I was foxed I took Dilys home. She made quite certain of that."

"She has been after you for some time, as I expect you are well aware."

"She made it very clear," the Duke said, "and because I was in what you might call a 'receptive mood,' I agreed to everything she suggested."

"She is not only beautiful," Eddie said, "but as bad as they come."

"That is what makes me apprehensive. She is trying to marry me."

"That is nothing new," Eddie replied. "They all want to marry you, and who shall blame them? There are not many handsome Dukes lying about on the beach."

"Eddie, I am being serious."

"About Dilys? You cannot be expected to take her seriously."

The Duke was silent for a moment. Then he said:

"Quite frankly, I cannot remember what I said last night."

"Does it matter very much?"

"I have a feeling that Dilys will not only make the most of what I did say but will make up what I did not."

The way the Duke spoke made Eddie lean forward in his chair with an incredulous expression on his face.

"Are you telling me, Vian," he asked, "that you are really worried about Dilys Chertsey? Good Heavens! With her reputation she could hardly expect to marry anybody like you."

"Well, I think she will attempt to," the Duke said, "and quite frankly, I do not want a scandal of that sort at this particular moment."

There was silence until Eddie said:

"What you are saying is, despite your air of bravado last night, you are not particularly pleased at being turned out of Buckingham Palace neck and crop."

"All right, if you want the truth, it is something which will upset my relatives more than anything that has happened to me before."

Eddie was silent, knowing that in contrast to the way he behaved in London, the Duke was meticulous in not doing anything outrageous when he was at his ancestral home in Buckinghamshire, where with his mother living in the Dower House and numerous other relatives on the Estate he was almost a model of everything an aristocrat and land-owner should be.

Eddie had in fact often speculated about the two sides of his friend's character, thinking that only an extremely clever man could have kept a balance between what he was and what his relatives wanted him to be in such an astute manner.

Aloud he said:

"Now I am beginning to understand why you drank so much last night."

"It was stupid of me," the Duke admitted, "and I dislike distressing my mother, who is not in good health at the moment."

"Perhaps she will not know," Eddie said hopefully.

"One of my sisters who dislikes me is a Lady-of-the-Bedchamber," the Duke said briefly.

"Of course!" Eddie exclaimed. "She married that old bore, Osborne, who has always been jealous of you."

"Exactly!"

"I am sorry," Eddie said, "and I do see that trouble with Dilys in addition will do nothing to help."

"It certainly will not," the Duke replied, "and somehow I have to avoid it. The question is — how?"

"Are you asking me?" his friend enquired.

"That is why I asked you to come here at what you think is an indecently early hour."

Eddie took a last sip of his brandy.

"If Dilys Chertsey wants to marry you," he said, "she must by this time have had enough of fighting off the condemnation of her relatives as well as those sanctimonious old prigs who look down their noses at anybody as beautiful as she is."

"Women never fight fairly," the Duke said, "and they always win in the end."

"I suppose you are right," Eddie agreed, "and nothing could be better for Dilys, from the point of view of the Social World, than if she was married to you."

The Duke brought his clenched fist down violently on the table, making the cups rattle.

"Blast it! I have no wish to marry anyone," he exclaimed, "and least of all Dilys Chertsey!"

As he spoke he thought he could not imagine any worse fate than being married to a wife whose past lovers would fill a room and who would always be appearing and reappearing anywhere he took her.

The Duke had not thought seriously of marriage despite the fact that his relatives, and especially his mother, were always begging him to have an heir.

He had had a somewhat unfortunate affair when he was very young which had made him suspicious that any woman he approached with a view to matrimony would be interested only in his title and not in himself.

He supposed that was inevitable where anyone as socially distinguished as he was concerned.

At the same time, he had a horror of a cold, calculated, arranged marriage with a woman who would bore him even before he went to bed with her and undoubtedly even more once he had.

Although he never said so aloud, he was determined that he would marry only when he fell in love, or to put it more exactly, when he was sure a woman he fancied was genuinely in love with him.

Then he asked himself cynically how he could ever be sure that any woman was considering him as a man rather than as a Duke, and the answer was always extremely depressing.

To be married to somebody like Dilys Chertsey would be to offend everything that was not only fastidious but idealistic in him.

Although he had broken many of the laws of decency in one way or another, he had no intention of destroying completely the trust that some of his relatives still had in him as head of the family.

Slowly he told Eddie exactly what had happened the night before and his recollection of what he had heard Dilys say as he went from her room.

"I fell into bed when I got home," he went on, "and it was only this morning when I woke up that I remembered clearly what it was, and I am quite certain I am not mistaken."

"She cannot tie you to it."

"I do not trust her," the Duke said gloomily. "You know as well as I do that she will try, and that is when she will make trouble."

"You must prevent it," Eddie said.

"How?" the Duke asked for the second time.

Both men were silent, and now as if the Duke felt he needed some sustenance he rose to fetch a glass from the sideboard and poured himself out a small brandy.

"Come on, Eddie," he said. "You have never failed me yet in all the tight spots we have been in together."

As he spoke he remembered how at Eton, Eddie had helped him in through a back window when he had been out of bounds and returned after the House had been closed.

Once he had escaped from the Proctors at Oxford and Eddie had acted as a decoy while the Duke ran for safety.

And when they had been in the Army there had definitely been one occasion when he had saved his life.

As it happened, the Duke had returned the compliment, but that for the moment was not the point.

"Well?" he questioned at last when the silence between them became oppressive.

"The best thing you can do is to go to the country at once!" Eddie said.

"And what if Dilys follows me to Minster and makes a scene when I refuse to marry her? That would be disastrous!"

"A scene is the one thing you must avoid," Eddie said. "Dilys must have known how drunk you were last night and will expect you to say that you do not remember anything that happened. But it is important that she should not be able to remind you."

"Then what am I to do if she follows me home?" the Duke asked. "Hide in a cupboard or up the chimney?"

"You are being very obtuse, Vian," Eddie replied. "Minster is not the only property you own."

The Duke raised his eye-brows.

"Then where are you suggesting I go?"

"Good God! Nobody has a wider choice than you. You have houses all over the place! I was looking at the maps on the wall in your Estate Office the last time we were at Minster, and I had no idea until then how much

property you do own. On all those acres and acres of
land coloured green there must be a house of some
sort!"

There was a pause before the Duke said slowly:

"What you are suggesting, Eddie, is that I go
someplace where nobody would expect me to be. It is
an idea!"

"It is the only sensible idea," Eddie replied. "If
you go abroad, people will say that you are running
away. That is what those who are in trouble of any sort
always do."

"That is true," the Duke agreed.

"You have only to announce that you are visiting
one of your properties. Then it will be up to Dilys to
find out which one, and that could take her quite a
time."

"There is one thing about you, Eddie," the Duke
said, "you always know what is best for me. As it
happens, now that I come to think about it, it is a long
time since I have visited some of my houses to see that
they are being kept up to scratch.'"

"What is important is for you to disappear plausibly,"
Eddie said, "and not as if you were 'running to cover,'
which in fact is what you are doing."

"Very well," the Duke agreed. "Where shall I go?"

"Anywhere that is not too obvious."

For almost the first time since he had arrived he
saw the Duke smile.

"I was hoping you would come with me."

"I would like to," Eddie said 'but not today,
which is when you must leave"

"Today?"

"Of course! Dilys will be on the war-path, you may
be sure of that! If you are going to receive any overtures from her, she will call either just before luncheon
or just after, and you must already have left"

"It is impossible." the Duke began then checked
himself.

Instead he rang the little gold bell which stood beside him on the table.

The Butler instantly opened the door.

"You rang, Your Grace?"

"Send Mr. Garston to me."

"Very good, Your Grace."

Eddie sat back in his chair and gave a short laugh.

"Now I will watch the wheels set in motion," he said. "I have seen it happen before, and it always amuses me."

"I am glad somebody is amused!" the Duke said ironically. "Personally, I find the whole thing a damned bore!"

"Look upon it as an adventure!"

"How long do you think I should stay away?" the Duke enquired. "And how long will it be before you can join me?"

"I cannot come until the end of the week," Eddie said. "I have to ask the Colonel's permission to go on leave, and I have entered three of my own men for the Army Heavyweight Boxing Championships. I can hardly let them down by not being present, can I?"

"No, of course not," the Duke agreed.

"As soon as that is over, I will be with you. You will not be going to Land's End or John O'Groats, but even so, you can lend me one of your best teams."

"I suppose that is a threat!" the Duke said. "You can have the bays."

"Thank you," Eddie said. "I shall enjoy driving them. As I have already said, I do not want to go too far, not having your expertise or your endurance."

"Very well," the Duke said, "but you might prefer to travel by train."

"I am damned if I do!" Eddie remarked. "Filthy, stinking, new-fangled machinery does not appeal to me. Besides, I cannot believe even you would have a house on a direct railway-line."

The Duke laughed.

"Not yet, but I expect one day it will come."

"I only hope I am not here to see it," his friend said. "I have no desire to live when the horse is no longer supreme."

"Nor have I!" the Duke exclaimed. "So let us get back to where I should go."

As he spoke the door opened and his Secretary, Mr. Garston, who had been with him ever since he had inherited and who was in charge of all his private affairs, came into the room.

He was a man of about fifty with a permanently worried expression on his face, but, as both the Duke and Eddie knew, he was a born organiser and was responsible for the smooth running of everything his master possessed.

"Good-morning, Your Grace," Mr. Garston said respectfully as he stood beside the Duke's chair.

"I have to leave London immediately, Garston," the Duke said. "In fact, within the next hour or so."

The Secretary's expression did not change, he merely replied quietly:

"Where will Your Grace be going?"

"That is something I have not yet decided," the Duke said. "Where do I own a comfortable house which I have not visited recently and which does not require too many days' driving before I reach it?"

Mr. Garston thought for a moment. "Then he said:

"You have your Hunting Lodge in Leicestershire, Your Grace."

"I was there last winter," the Duke replied, "and found it, as you well know, extremely uncomfortable."

"The alterations which Your Grace suggested have been completed."

The Duke did not reply, obviously not pleased with the idea, and Mr. Garston said:

"You have a house which Your Grace has not visited since you were a very young man, and I have a feeling, perhaps erroneously, that you are not particularly interested in it."

"Which one are you talking about?" the Duke enquired.

"Queen's Hoo, Your Grace, in Worcestershire."

The Duke looked at him for a moment. Then he said:

"Queen's Hoo? I had almost forgotten I owned it."

"It is still yours, Your Grace."

"I have never heard you speak of Queen's Hoo," Eddie interposed. "An intriguing name."

"It was built for Queen Elizabeth as a retreat from her onerous duties in London," the Duke explained.

He gave a somewhat twisted smile before he added:

"It seems an appropriate place for me to go. Very well, Garston, I will go to Queen's Hoo. Send a groom ahead to warn them of my arrival. I will drive my Phaeton with four outriders, and one of the horses must be Perseus, so that I can ride when I wish to. The luggage can travel as usual in the brake drawn by six horses."

"Very good, Your Grace."

Without asking any more questions Mr. Garston went from the room.

Eddie laughed.

"Just like that!" he said. "Rub the magic lamp, the genie appears, you tell him your wishes, and everything happens!"

"I hope so," the Duke said. "I have not been at Queen's Hoo since I was twenty. My grandmother lived there until she died. She quarrelled with my father and refused to live in the Dower House at Minster. I used to enjoy staying there. I only hope the place has not changed."

"You will very likely find it overgrown and with the staff out of hand and the tenants in revolt. Absent masters deserve all they get!" Eddie teased.

"Well, at least it will give me something to do to put it to rights," the Duke replied, "but I am going to be damned bored until you arrive."

"Then you must repent of your sins."

"That is something I have no intention of doing, although it would undoubtedly please Her Majesty if she thought that was what I was reduced to."

"This was bound to happen sooner or later, and at least you have had a run for your money."

"You sound as if you are condemning me," the Duke expostulated.

"Not exactly."

"What do you mean by that?"

"If you want the truth," Eddie replied, "in many ways you are wasting your good brain on pursuing enjoyment which is hardly worth the cost when you tot it up the next morning."

For a moment the Duke looked annoyed.

"That is certainly a condemnation."

"Well, you asked me," Eddie answered, "and we have always told each other the truth."

"I had no idea that like everybody else you were criticising me."

"Not really," Eddie said. "It is only that I think it is a mistake for any party to go on too long."

"Now I think you are talking sense," the Duke agreed.

He suddenly pushed back his chair and said:

"Dammit all, Eddie! You are making me depressed. The party is not over. I intend to enjoy myself for a very long time yet before I 'settle down,' as my relatives call it."

"You have sown a fine harvest of wild oats already!"

"Curse you, you are sermonising again," the Duke complained. "The sooner I get off on this 'goose-chase' away from you, from the Palace, and from Dilys, the better and the sooner I can come back."

"The return of the Prodigal!" Eddie laughed. "Although I do not suppose, being you, you will eat many husks, and there will be a number of pretty milkmaids who will tumble over themselves at the sight of you."

"I am fed up with your croaking," the Duke said. "Go back to Barracks and your Champion Pugilists."

Eddie laughed again and finished off his brandy.

"I will let Garston know as soon as I am able to join you," he said. "And mind you make certain there is something more amusing waiting for me than dancing round the Maypole!"

"You will doubtless find me sitting in 'sackcloth and ashes,' contemplating my navel like an Indian Fakir," the Duke replied.

"I will take a bet of one-hundred-to-one against that!"

The Duke smiled.

"Then you will win! I promise you I am a very impenitent penitent! Make sure nobody knows where I have gone!"

"I shall start by telling everybody that you are at Minster," Eddie said, "and after they have found out that Buckinghamshire has not seen you, I shall suggest all your other properties, one by one."

"Be certain that Dilys does not get the truth out of you," the Duke warned.

"You may be sure of that," Eddie replied. "When we parted it was acrimoniously, and it is no good ever looking back."

The Duke stared at Eddie for a moment. Then the inference of what his friend had said sank into his mind.

"Damn you, Eddie!" he said. "For that reason, if for no other, I shall make absolutely certain I do not marry Dilys!"

Chapter Two

The Duke spent what he considered was an uncomfortable night at a Posting-Inn near Oxford.

Ordinarily he would have stayed at Blenheim Palace with the Duke of Marlborough, but when Mr. Garston suggested it, he told his Secretary that the journey was secret and nobody was to know where he was going.

Mr. Garston was too well trained to look surprised.

The Duke made it clear that the servants were not to talk in the Inns which they frequented after work and that none of his friends were to have any idea that if he was in the country he was not at Minster.

The Duke always travelled with everything that appertained to his comfort.

He slept in his own bed-linen, ate with his own silver cutlery, and one of his outriders who was an experienced Chef cooked the dishes the way he liked them in the kitchens at the Inns.

All the same, after only a few hours' sleep following the excesses of the night before, he awoke to lie in the darkness feeling depressed.

He was intelligent enough to realise that this was because he was facing a few days entirely alone without the companionship either of any close men-friends or of a beautiful woman.

Thinking back, he could not remember when such a situation had occurred before, and he told himself

23

that he would be hideously bored and the sooner Eddie arrived the better.

Furthermore, he decided that even Eddie would not relieve what would undoubtedly be a long-drawn-out stay with nothing to do.

"I would far better have gone abroad," he told himself.

He believed that the French Capital, at any rate, would have provided him with the sort of amusement that had become a part of his life.

He had found on his last visit that the "Courtesans," which was a polite word for them, had an experienced allure that could not be found in any other Capital.

'Frenchwomen know their business,' the Duke had thought at the time, and it occurred to him now that what he needed was a French mistress to wile away the weary hours he must spend at Queen's Hoo with nothing to do in the evenings but read.

Not that he disliked reading. The Duke was in fact an extremely well-read man. But every mile he drove away from London he was resenting that the Queen should exile him not only from Buckingham Palace but from his habitual routine, thereby disrupting his whole way of life.

He was ready to blame the Queen, but he knew that at least fifty per cent of the present situation was his own fault by becoming involved with Dilys Chertsey.

The mere thought of her made him set his lips in a hard line. He tried to tell himself that his suspicions might prove to be unfounded and that owing to the wine befogging his brain he might have misunderstood what she had said. But in his heart of hearts he doubted it.

He knew that to be optimistic was to be unrealistic and that Eddie was right in saying he must take no chances where Dilys was concerned.

As the hours that he lay awake passed slowly, he rose before dawn to write a short note.

He told Eddie not only to hurry to join him with all possible speed but to bring with him two "charmers" who would help to pass the time more pleasantly than if they were alone.

The Duke gave it some thought before he added the names of two women. One was an extremely attractive half-French, half-Hungarian whom he had been thinking of taking under his protection.

He had noticed her first when he was riding in the Park and thought that she was attractive and that her face had a slight air of mystery about it, due undoubtedly to her dual nationality.

But it was not only her face he noticed, but the way she rode and the elegance of her habit.

It was only after enquiring who she was that he learnt that her appearance and her horsemanship were very much part of her "stock in trade."

There were establishing themselves in London a number of women who broke in the horses that filled the Livery Stables.

Although most gentlemen with means brought their own horses to London, there was always a demand for more, especially for the wives and daughters, and the Livery Stables let out horses which were not only finely bred but also well trained.

However, many ladies who thought it fashionable to ride were nervous when they were on horseback, and quite a number of young women from the country were making a good living from ensuring that the horses that were hired out were docile.

The Livery Stables quickly advanced from providing horses in this category to finding that an attractive woman riding a superlative horse that was for sale could put up the price.

The Duke learnt that one of the most reliable Livery Stables in Mayfair showed off its horses in the Park with women who were not only as eye-catching as the animal on which they were mounted, but who also when it came to hard bargaining were as expensive.

The Duke had taken Gigi, for that was her name, out to dinner and discovered that she had a stimulating wit which was undoubtedly due to her French mother, while the way she rode could be a heritage from her Hungarian father.

He had made no suggestions at the time, but he was well aware that if he should offer Gigi a house he owned in Chelsea, which was for the moment unoccupied, she would be only too eager to accept it.

But where his mistresses were concerned he never acted hastily.

He knew better than anybody else how quickly he could grow bored and indifferent to a woman who at first attracted him and whom he had found desirable.

When this occurred with any of the Social Beauties, who were invariably married, it was easy to say good-bye or often to simply drift away without there being many scenes or recriminations.

In nearly every case the lady concerned would feel too humiliated and too proud to do anything but cry at losing a man she had loved.

But she would also try to show, as far as the rest of the world was concerned, that she was not heart-broken and the break had been of her own choosing.

His experience with women of another class was rather different.

The Duke had found that while by all the unwritten laws a mistress should accept her dismissal in a philosophical spirit and merely ensure that the pay-off was a generous one, where he was concerned the rules "went by the board."

His mistresses always became excessively feminine and not only declared that he had broken their hearts but became noisily jealous because they had been supplanted in his affections.

As often as not, they were violently aggressive in refusing to believe that he no longer wanted them.

"Why am I so different from every other man?" the Duke had asked himself time and time again.

But he would not have been human if he had not realised that it was because all women, whatever their class or position in life, found him an irresistible lover and invariably fought like tigresses to keep him from leaving them.

This had meant that the house in Chelsea was more often empty than filled, and the Duke wondered now whether he would be foolish to instal another occupant.

At the same time, he knew that Gigi was undoubtedly very attractive and he told himself that he would be safer with a professional than with an enthusiastic amateur like Dilys, who had ambitions of marrying him.

Anyway, he was quite certain that Gigi would jump at the suggestion of coming with Eddie to stay with him in the country.

He had noticed another very pretty rider in the same Livery Stable who he thought would amuse Eddie, unless he preferred to choose his own female companion.

They had been such close friends for so long that the Duke knew Eddie's taste as well as he knew his own, and he thought that Bettsy, who was sprightly, vivacious, and very pretty, would with her golden hair and blue eyes be a perfect foil to Gigi's dark beauty.

"They will cheer things up considerably," he told himself as he wrote his signature with a flourish.

He sealed his letter, put it ready to send by Post-Chaise first thing in the morning, and returned to bed.

Finally he slept peacefully until his Valet called him at eight o'clock, and half-an-hour later he was eating a large breakfast cooked by his own servant before he set off towards Queen's Hoo.

It was a sunny day and he started early before it became too hot. As it had showered with rain in the night, the dust was not oppressive and the Duke appreciated the beauty of the countryside, the Cotswold Hills, the green fields, some golden with buttercups, the hedgerows brilliant with dog-roses, and the fragrance of honeysuckle.

He made Broadway in record time and was just pulling up at the Inn where he intended to have luncheon when he saw to his surprise a servant standing outside wearing his own livery.

As he drew his horses to a standstill, the Duke recognised one of his own grooms and realised that the man in question must have been the messenger whom Mr. Garston had sent ahead to inform his household at Queen's Hoo that he was on his way.

"What has happened?" he asked sharply as the man hurried to the side of the Phaeton.

"I'm sorry, Your Grace," the man said, "but I could get no farther."

"Why not?"

"Rufus went lame, Your Grace, just as I were arriving here. I've called a Vet to 'im, but 'e can't be moved for a few days."

The Duke's lips tightened.

He disliked his plans going awry, but he was sure it had not been the groom's fault, knowing that those he employed in his stables were very strictly supervised and all of them could be trusted with his valuable horses.

He knotted his reins and stepped down, listening as he did so to the groom's nervous explanation of what had occurred.

Then before he did anything else he went to the stables to inspect Rufus.

He realised without being told that the horse had strained a tendon in one of his back legs and he knew it would be no use to ride him until it was completely healed.

He told the groom what to do and how to treat it, and then, sweeping aside the man's stammered apologies for not having carried out Mr. Garston's instructions, went into the Inn for luncheon.

He was not seriously perturbed by the unforeseen

incident, for he had always left instructions that every house he owned should be ready at only a few hours' notice to receive him and any guests he might wish to bring with him.

It was twelve years since he had visited Queen's Hoo, but he knew that Mr. Garston kept a very strict eye on the managers and agents on every Estate he owned, and he was quite certain that the house would be well staffed.

If it was not, he would have a great deal to say in the matter.

In the meantime he dismissed the minor catastrophe from his mind and concentrated on his luncheon, which was excellent. He then drove on, enjoying the scenery and the distant view of the Malvern Hills silhouetted against the sky.

He had not hurried over luncheon, and it was late in the afternoon before he knew he was within a mile or two of Queen's Hoo.

At this stage of his journey he was alone, for after luncheon he had ordered Perseus to be saddled and ready outside the front door of the Inn, and he had ridden away from his entourage across country over land that he recognized.

He had in fact often hunted over it when he had stayed with his grandmother.

The Duke found that Perseus, who was still fresh despite the miles he had travelled in the morning, provided him with exercise which raised his spirits and swept away the depression he had felt in the night.

As he had his first sight of the house which was a part of his growing up, he realised that because he had ridden as the crow flew he would be there before any of his servants.

Although the brake was drawn by six horses he had been amused to notice when they left London how much luggage it contained.

He knew this was due to Mr. Garston's care for his comfort, but it had undoubtedly slowed down the vehicle, besides the fact that it also conveyed a number of servants besides his Valet.

He passed through a copse of beech trees, then pulled in his horse to look at the house to which he had returned with a feeling of wild excitement in the School holidays and with a deeper pleasure as he grew older.

The plan of Queen's Hoo, which had been built for Queen Elizabeth, was, as was traditional, in the shape of an "E."

Its red bricks had mellowed with the years and it was now a warm, exquisitely beautiful pink, with its diamond-paned windows glittering like jewels in the afternoon sun.

Over the front door was carved the regalia of the Queen, and because she had decreed that it was to be her special abode and to bear her name, the Minsters who had built it for her and their descendents had Her Majesty's permission to fly the Royal standard on the rooftop.

The Duke recalled how proud he had been of this privilege when he was a small boy and how he had boasted of it to his friends at School and in consequence had been kicked by the Prefects for being conceited.

But Queen's Hoo was certainly something to be conceited about, and he thought now as he looked at it that he had forgotten how beautiful it was and how it had a dream-like quality that he had never found in any of his other houses.

He knew that the reason why he had not returned before was that his grandmother was no longer there, whom he had loved, although he had never admitted it, more than his own mother or any of his other relations, and he could not face the house without her.

And yet now he thought he had been foolish, and she might even have been hurt to know that he had neglected a house which had meant so much to him when he was young.

His father, like so many men, had resented and in fact been jealous of his son, who had therefore never been really happy at home. It was his mother, because she loved him, who had suggested sending him to his grandmother at Queen's Hoo for the holidays to keep him out of his father's way.

The Duke remembered that he had at first resented being sent away from Minster but soon had become overwhelmingly glad.

His grandmother was a very intelligent and at the same time sympathetic woman, and after she had quarrelled with her eldest son she had found it intolerable to live in the Dower House of Minster, where she had once reigned supreme.

A great beauty, she had been successful in surrounding herself with all the best brains of the period, and to be a friend of the "Duchess Sheila" was considered almost the equivalent of being in residence at a University.

The lavish entertainments arranged by the Duchess in London were surpassed only by her important house-parties at Minster.

When the Duke was staying with her at Queen's Hoo he would listen to the stories she told him of the Kings and Princes and Prime Ministers and Statesmen who had gathered round the dining-table in the big Banqueting-Hall.

They either, she had said, made their laughter ring up to the lofty painted ceiling or made history as they discussed the affairs of nations over their port and brandy.

"Sometimes I thought, dearest child," she had said to her grandson, "I changed the map of Europe by getting two antagonists together and forcing them to understand each other's point of view. I remember two occasions when I undoubtedly prevented a war."

It had all been fascinating to the Duke, and although he did not realise it at the time, it had taught him history from a personal angle, geography, and diplomacy in a way which no master could impart it and which was to stand him in good stead as he grew older.

'Yes,' he thought now, 'the reason I have not returned is that Queen's Hoo could never be the same without Grandmama.'

At the same time he now felt eager to see it, and spurring Perseus on he rode down a short incline and entered the orchard which led to the gardens at the back of the house.

Deep in his memories of the past, the Duke suddenly knew he had no wish to arrive without warning and have to explain his presence to an astonished staff.

His own servants could do that, and he thought that in the meantime, as he was undoubtedly well ahead of them, he would see if the garden was as he remembered it and had not been neglected.

He rode through the apple trees which were in blossom and saw the high Elizabethan brick wall which he knew protected the Herb Garden and beside it, enclosing the green lawns, the ancient yew-hedge with its fine examples of topiary work.

He reached the end of the orchard and knew he must explore the rest on foot. He therefore dismounted, knotting the reins securely in front of the saddle, and let Perseus go loose.

Perseus had been his favourite horse for three years, and it always pleased the Duke that while he could be difficult, tricky, and hard to handle with anybody else, with him he was a model of obedience.

If he whistled Perseus came to him, and as he patted the horse's neck now he knew that Perseus would not wander too far and would come as soon as he was called.

The Duke walked along the outside of the topiary hedge to where he knew there was a wrought-iron gate leading into the Herb Garden, and when he tried it he was relieved to find that it was not locked.

The Herb Garden seemed in perfect order. It had been a source of great pride to his grandmother that she could grow exactly the same herbs which were

listed in the chronicles of the house as having been
planted in 1562.

Between low box-hedges ran little paths made of
bricks laid skilfully in a pattern. They were well weed-
ed, and the Duke walked along them thinking he would
certainly commend the gardeners if the condition of the
rest of the garden was as good as this.

Another gate brought him out onto the smooth
lawns edged by beds of herbaceous flowers grown in
front of the topiary hedges.

Here the Duke hesitated, wondering if he should
turn right, towards the house, or left, towards what
would have been the Water Garden.

Beyond it were the shrubberies and beyond them
were the woods which protected the house. They rose
up the slopes of a hill to where at the peak there was a
special look-out from which one could survey the countryside and the Estate for many miles.

'I must go there soon,' the Duke thought, but it
was a stiff climb and could keep.

Suddenly conscious of the warmth of the sunshine
and that he had been riding for some hours, he took off
his tall hat and felt not only the heat of the sun on his
face but a faint breeze coming from the trees.

It was very pleasant and the Duke felt as if already
the peace, or perhaps the right word was "magic," of
Queen's Hoo was sweeping away the feelings of tension
and irritation which had been with him ever since he
had talked to the Lord Chamberlain.

He walked on and found as he expected the Water
Garden with its tiny trickling cascade, its rare plants in
bloom, which he remembered had come from the
Botanical Gardens at Kew and many other parts of the
world.

Also in the little pool below the cascade under the
water-lilies there were flashes of red and gold as gold-
fish like those he had loved when he was small swam
round it.

He felt almost childishly pleased that everything was unchanged, and leaving the Water Garden he walked along a narrow mossy path bordered on each side with azaleas and rhododendrons just coming into bloom to where he knew there was a small Grecian Temple.

This had been added long after the house had been built; in fact, it had been a trophy stolen from Greece by the first Duke of Ilminster in the early years of the Eighteenth Century.

But because it was so beautiful and classically perfect it had seemed to fit in as if the garden had been designed for it.

The Duke thought it had in fact been one of the main works of art to shape his taste and inspire him to become a collector as his forebears had been.

As he walked on he found himself quoting Lord Byron:

> *"The isles of Greece, the isles of Greece!*
> *Where burning Sappho loved and sung,*
> *Where grew the arts of war and peace . . ."*

It was a long time since he had read those lines, and yet he thought now that it was the Greek Temple and perhaps Byron himself who had inspired in him a desire to know more of the "arts of war and peace" and to find them not only in things but in people.

The idea amused him and he was smiling as he came upon the Temple itself.

It was quite small and very simple, and to the Duke it seemed to glow in its white purity as if it were a jewel.

Then, as instinctively he stood still a little way from it, he realised there was somebody else in it.

For the moment, because he was happy to be alone with his memories and to feel the unusual emotions that Queen's Hoo had aroused in him, he was annoyed.

Then he saw that seated on the steps of the Temple and leaning against one of its white pillars was a woman.

The Duke saw first her gown, which because it was white blended with the Temple itself, then the flowers which were loose on her lap.

Then as he took a step forward he could see that her head was resting against the pillar and she was asleep.

He moved farther forward, and now he was aware that he was looking at a girl who was quite young, although he thought that because her eyes were closed perhaps she looked younger than she actually was in years.

She had a small heart-shaped face, and the lashes which rested on her cheeks were dark at the roots but as they curled backwards were golden at the tips like those of a very young child.

The gold of her hair was so fair that it seemed almost to blend with the patina of the ancient marble pillar.

The Duke stood looking down at the intruder, wondering who on earth she could be.

She was certainly very lovely, and he thought with a touch of amusement that he had in fact found the "Sleeping Beauty," which was very appropriate to Queen's Hoo.

Never had there been any female influence in his life there except that of his grandmother.

Now he knew, as he thought about it, that Queen's Hoo was a house made for romance, and he wondered why he had never come here before with one of the many women whom he had found attractive and with whom he had wanted to be alone somewhere and to talk of love.

But none of them, he thought, were in the least like the girl sleeping on the steps of the Greek Temple.

For a moment he wondered if in fact he was dreaming and although she seemed part of the Temple itself she would disappear and he would find himself alone with his memories.

Then he thought that he was being ridiculously imaginative, which was very unlike his usual attitude towards life and in particular towards women.

His curiosity as to who the intruder could be made him move a little nearer and then sit down beside her on the steps of the Temple.

As he did so, he caught the spur of his boot against the lower step and the slight noise made the sleeper open her eyes.

As she did so, the Duke was just seating himself, which brought him nearer to her than he would have been otherwise, and she looked up directly into his face.

He was aware of two large, strangely coloured eyes, and he heard her say in a very soft voice as she stared at him hazily, still half-asleep:

"I was... dreaming of... you."

The Duke seated himself beside her and asked:

"Of me? That is surprising!"

She moved her head from the pillar and looked at him in a way which told him that she was wondering if he was real. Then she said:

"I... I was... asleep... who are you?"

"I was about to ask you the same question," the Duke replied. "But then I knew you must be the 'Sleeping Beauty.'"

She smiled.

"It seems very lazy to be asleep at this time of the day, but I was up so early and there has been so much to do."

The Duke wondered how there could be so much to do in Queen's Hoo when the household was not yet aware of his arrival.

He was just about to tell her who he was, when he thought that would be a mistake and he should find out what was happening before he revealed his identity.

"If I behaved as I ought to have done," he said, "I should have awakened you with a kiss!"

She gave a completely unselfconscious little laugh.

"That is what one would expect in story-books," she replied, "but in real life it could not happen."

"Why not?" the Duke asked.

"Because you would not kiss somebody you had never seen before, and I would have to have been shocked and angry."

The Duke thought this was not the answer he would have received from anybody else if he had suggested kissing them or even if he did kiss them, and he replied:

"Well, as I have not shocked you or made you angry, perhaps you will tell me who you are and why you have been so busy on this particular day."

"You are a stranger," she replied, "so you would not know that this is the anniversary of the day that the building of Queen's Hoo was finished. So it is the birthday of the house, and a very special day for those of us who live here."

She spoke with a note in her voice that told the Duke she was entirely sincere.

Looking back into the past, he remembered that his grandmother had told him that on this particular day of the year she always placed flowers in front of Queen Elizabeth's portrait in the Great Hall.

"We must thank Her Majesty," the Duchess had said, "because she had asked for Queen's Hoo to be built and the Minster who had been living on another part of the Estate at the time carried out the Queen's wishes."

"So you have been picking flowers," the Duke said after a moment's pause, "to commemorate the birthday of a house as if it were a person."

"The birthday of this house is more important than the birthday of any person could ever be," the girl replied. "Can you not understand what Queen's Hoo has meant to all those who have lived here for nearly three centuries? It has been their home, has given them shelter and love and an inspiration which has reached out in a way which I believe has changed the lives of people in this country and perhaps in other parts of the world."

The Duke thought this might almost be his grandmother speaking, and he asked:

"And why should this matter to you?"

"I live here!"

The Duke looked at her in astonishment, feeling that this was something that Mr. Garston should have told him; or if he had done so, he had no memory of it.

"You live here with your parents?" he asked slowly.

He thought as he spoke that perhaps she was the daughter of the Housekeeper, the Agent, or somebody else in his employment.

The girl shook her head.

"No," she said. "I was all alone in the world, but now I am part of Queen's Hoo, and because I love it, it belongs to me."

She got up as she spoke, holding her flowers carefully in her hands.

"I must go!" she said. "If you follow the path up through the woods you will get to the look-out, which I expect is what you wish to find. As it happens, you should not have come into the garden because you are trespassing."

Before the Duke could speak, she smiled and added:

"But because this is a very special day you will be forgiven."

Then she turned swiftly with the grace of a young fawn and started to move away with what seemed incredible swiftness over the green lawns.

"Wait! Wait!" the Duke called.

But by the time he had found his voice she was out of sight, and as he rose to his feet very much more slowly than she had done, he saw her already far away in the distance.

Her fair hair was gleaming in the sunshine, and the full skirts of her white gown moved with a grace as if she floated rather than ran over the velvet lawns.

"In God's name, who can she be?" the Duke asked himself, and knew it was a puzzle to which he must find the answer.

* * *

The Duke sat in the Grecian Temple for some time, thinking it would be a good idea to let the excitement and commotion of his servants' arrival settle down before he appeared.

Then he went back the way he had come through the Herb Garden to find Perseus and rode him through the orchard and along the front of the house, skirting the side of the stream before he rode towards the stables.

The stream where the Duke had caught trout as a small boy, and where he had swum when he was hot in the summer and had learnt to control a punt when he was older, was unchanged.

The irises in bloom were growing profusely along its banks, and the bridge which one had to cross before one reached the house seemed to have grown smaller with time.

The sun was sparkling on the water, and the swans moving serenely with their baby cygnets following behind them were all part of his memories.

The entrance to the stables was unchanged too, except for the climbing ivy that almost obscured the stonework, and the cobbled yard looked more worn than it had years ago.

As he expected, he found that his grooms were already there, the horses from both the brake and the Phaeton now in their stalls.

When Perseus was led away from him he turned

and walked to the front of the house to enter by the main door.

This door was now at the side of the house because his grandmother had thought the huge Elizabethan Hall which occupied almost the whole of the centre block of the house should be used as a Sitting-Room rather than a place of reception.

Although the external appearance of the front of the house was unchanged, one entered now at the side and walked along a wide passage decorated with armour of the Elizabethan period.

This led into the Great Hall, which the Duke thought was more impressive than the Hall of any other house he had ever seen.

The ceiling was very high, the carved stone fireplace magnificent, and the walls which did not carry shields, cutlasses, pikes, and many other weapons were hung with pictures that had all been painted during the Queen's reign.

The Duke wondered now, although he had never thought of it before, why he had never moved such valuable and fine paintings to one of his houses which he visited more frequently.

Then he knew that to remove or alter any part of Queen's Hoo would be a crime.

The first thing he saw as he entered the Hall was that not only did the painting of Queen Elizabeth have flowers in front of it but the carved frame also was decorated with them.

He looked round and found that the frames of her Courtiers and Statesmen, three of them being Minsters, on other walls were also beflowered.

On the long refectory-table in the centre, at which once the Queen herself had enjoyed her food, there was an enormous vase of exquisitely arranged flowers, which, like the decoration of the frames, the Duke was certain owed its artistry to his "Sleeping Beauty."

He walked to the fireplace to stand with his back to it, looking round the room and thinking of how often he had sat here talking to his grandmother, reading, or entertaining his friends who had always been welcome.

He recalled even more vividly his dogs. There had been two of them, who followed him everywhere he went, and he felt now that if he looked down he would find one of them looking up at him eagerly as if he begged to be taken out walking or shooting.

'I can see this is going to be a journey back in time,' the Duke thought, and tried to laugh cynically to himself but found it surprisingly difficult.

Hurrying into the Hall came an old man with white hair whom it took him a moment to recognise as Barker, the Butler who had served his grandmother.

"This, Your Grace, is a great surprise!" the man exclaimed, and as he reached him the Duke remembered his name.

"Nice to see you, Barker!" he exclaimed.

"I've been hoping and praying, Master Vian—I mean, Your Grace—you'd come and visit us one day," the Butler said.

"Well, I am here," the Duke smiled, "and I expect you have been told that a groom was sent to warn you of my arrival but was unable to complete the journey because his horse went lame."

" 'Twas unfortunate, very unfortunate, Your Grace, but it won't be difficult for us to make you comfortable, and it'll be like the old days to have you here, Your Grace—just like the old days!"

The Duke was uncomfortably aware that there was a tremble in Barker's voice and a suspicious moisture in his eyes, and he instinctively shied away from anything that was sentimental.

"I would like a drink, Barker," he said.

"Of course, Your Grace. It's coming, and I hopes we've a claret that's to Your Grace's liking."

As Barker spoke, a footman appeared with a silver tray on which was a decanter and placed it on a table in the corner where the Duke remembered the wine had always been placed in the past.

He accepted a glass of claret as Barker explained to him that the champagne would have to be chilled before he could drink it, then he said casually:

"The flowers are very charming, but as you did not know I was arriving, I cannot believe they are in my honour."

"No, no, Your Grace. It's the birthday of the house, as Your Grace must remember."

"Yes, of course, I remember now," the Duke replied, "but who has arranged them?"

"I have!" a voice said from the other end of the Hall before Barker could speak, and the girl the Duke had seen sleeping on the Temple steps came towards him.

He waited unto she reached his side and curtseyed before he said:

"We can now introduce ourselves."

"I am Fabia Wilton, Your Grace," she replied, "and I think it was very unkind of you to let me think you were a stranger trespassing on your own land!"

She then hesitated and looked to see if the servants were still there. But they had withdrawn, and seeing that she and the Duke were alone she looked up at him and said in a worried voice:

"May I . . . speak to Your Grace? I feel that I should . . . explain my . . . presence here."

"I am delighted to listen to anything you have to say to me," the Duke answered.

"I only hope . . . after what I have to . . . say you will not . . . want me to go . . . away."

"Why should I do that?"

"Because . . . and perhaps it was . . . wrong . . . Mr. Durwood did not inform either Your Grace or Mr. Garston that I was . . . living here."

Mr. Durwood managed the Estate and the Duke thought it was decidedly strange that he should have allowed somebody to live at Queen's Hoo without his knowledge, since it was certainly his duty to report anything of the kind.

But the Duke was at the moment too curious to be annoyed.

"I think you must explain what has happened from the very beginning," he said. "May I offer you a glass of wine, or perhaps you should be offering it to me."

"Now you are being unkind," Fabia replied.

She gave a little sigh.

"How could I imagine for one moment when I first saw you that you were the Duke? But now I see that you are as I expected you would be.."

"You told me you were dreaming of me."

A faint flush appeared in Fabia's cheeks and she looked away from him.

She did not answer and after a moment he said:

"As I suggested, I think you should start at the beginning."

"Yes . . . of course."

"Suppose you sit down?"

She obeyed him, sitting like a child on the edge of a chair, her full skirts spread out, her hands in her lap.

She looked up at him with a worried expression in her eyes, which he now saw were green flecked with gold and so large that they seemed to dominate the whole of her small face.

The Duke knew he had been right in thinking she was beautiful, but in a different way from anybody he had seen before.

Once again he had the feeling that she was not real and might at any moment vanish and he would find himself alone in the Great Hall.

Then as the silence became almost embarrassing he walked across to the table to pour himself a little more wine, saying as he did so:

"I am listening to everything you have to tell me, and needless to say I am curious as to what it will be."

"We . . . came to live in the Manor House the year before the Duchess, your grandmother . . . died," Fabia began.

"Who is 'we'?" the Duke questioned.

"My father, my mother, and myself."

"Why did you choose the Manor?"

"We were looking for a house, and because my mother was a distant relative of your family, your grandmother suggested we should live near her."

"Your mother was a Minster?" the Duke questioned.

"No, not as near as that," Fabia replied, "but her grandmother was one, and I have always been very, very proud that I have Minster blood in my veins. Perhaps that is why I feel so much love and affection for Queen's Hoo."

She spoke with such a note of sincerity in her voice that the Duke thought it strange that the house should mean so much to any young woman.

But he did not wish to side-track her from her story, so he said:

"Perhaps you should tell me your father's full name."

"He was Colonel Gerald Wilton, and he was in the Grenadiers until he was wounded and had to leave the Regiment."

Fabia paused for a moment before she said:

"We did not have very much money after that, and I think that was when Mama wrote to your grandmother asking if she knew of a house they could rent which would not be too expensive."

"And so you came to the Manor. I remember the house," the Duke said.

"We were happy there, but Papa was never strong after he was wounded, and he died about five years after the Duchess."

There was a little break in her voice that told the Duke how much she minded losing her father, and quickly, because he was afraid she too might become sentimental, he asked:

"What happened then?"

"Mama and I lived at the Manor until two years ago, when I was sixteen, and then . . . Mama died . . ."

Fabia looked at him and the Duke knew what she was going to say next and said it for her:

"So you came to Queen's Hoo!"

"I had nowhere else to go except to relations who live very far away in the North of Scotland and whom I have never seen . . . and I think I have some . . . cousins in Northumberland."

"Who was it that suggested you should come here?"

"I think, to be honest, I suggested it myself," Fabia replied. "I asked Mr. Durwood if I could perhaps work in the house, mending the curtains which needed repairing, which Mama and I had often done anyway. We could not bear to see such beautiful embroidery becoming frayed or torn."

She looked at the Duke pleadingly again and he said:

"And what did Mr. Durwood reply?"

"He said that Hannah and I could come here. We would be no trouble and you would not mind."

"Who is Hannah?"

"She was my Nurse when I was small. Then when Papa was wounded and we could not afford any other servants, she did everything."

"So she is here with you."

"She works too, and we have repaired all the embroidered bed-spreads in the State-Rooms . . . relined the curtains on the beds . . . and I have repaired the embroidered stools in a Tudor design, as Mama taught me how to do. I promise you . . . we really have been . . . useful!"

There was so much anxiety and apprehension in the young, hesitating voice that the Duke felt he could not go on keeping her in the suspense of wondering if he would be angry and turn her out.

"I am sure you have earned your keep a dozen times over," he said, "and may I make it clear that I welcome you as a guest at Queen's Hoo."

He saw the colour come into her face and the

sudden sparkle in her eyes and knew how apprehensive she had been.

"Do you mean...that? Do you...really mean it?" she asked. "If I had to leave I would not only be...very frightened because we have...nowhere else to go...but I think also it would...break my heart!"

"Does Queen's Hoo mean so much to you?"

"Everything! Do you not understand? Nobody could live here and not be happy. To me it is not just a home...it is much more than...that."

"In what way?" he enquired.

As if he was being too inquisitive, she looked away from him. He knew she was not going to give him a truthful answer but was searching for words with which to parry his question.

It struck him that perhaps she was in love with somebody who was also living in the house. He wondered who it could be and decided it would not be difficult for him to find out sooner or later.

"So one of your tasks," he said, "has been to arrange the flowers, or is it perhaps only on special occasions like today that you make the effort?"

"I always put flowers in all the main rooms!" Fabia replied. "You could come here on any other day and see them. Even at Christmas we manage to find enough flowers from the greenhouses for the Hall and the Drawing-Room."

The Duke noticed the use of the word "we" and could not help feeling amused that this girl was so closely identified with his house that it seemed as much hers as his.

Then it struck him that perhaps the fact that everything he had seen so far in the house seemed to be in perfect condition, just as the garden was exactly as it had been when his grandmother was alive, was due entirely to Fabia.

He was well aware that when houses were left unoccupied and ignored by their owners, those who served in them became discouraged and found it impossible to do their best.

At the same time, he was not going to compliment or encourage her in the belief that she owned the place until he knew a great deal more.

She rose to her feet.

"May I go and tell Hannah that Your Grace is not turning us out?" she asked. "She has always felt uneasy about coming here, and when she heard you had arrived she was most upset."

"Where was she suggesting you go to?" the Duke asked.

Fabia smiled and for the first time since he had known her there was a hint of mischief in her eyes.

"I think, as we have very little money, Hannah felt that the only solution to our problem would be to hide in a hay-stack until you had left."

The Duke laughed.

"But I am very . . . very glad that we can stay," Fabia said. "Thank you . . . thank you very . . . very much for being so . . . k-kind!"

The words spilled out of her lips as if they came from her heart, and the Duke found her gratitude very touching.

"Shall I say that I am delighted for you to be here," he said. "I was rather afraid of being bored all by myself."

Fabia looked at him in surprise.

"Are you saying . . . that you want to . . . see me . . . and talk to me?" she asked. "Hannah said I was to . . . stay in my own room and not intrude."

"If you do that," the Duke said, "I shall have to order you to keep me company. If there is one thing I dislike, it is being bored, and to prevent that, Miss Wilton, will certainly be one of your duties."

Fabia gave a little cry of delight.

"That will be very exciting for me," she said, "and certainly not a duty, Your Grace, but a very great pleasure!"

Again she was speaking with an undeniable sincerity. Then she gave him a little curtsey and added:

"I must go and tell Hannah, or she will have packed everything we possess."

She gave the Duke a flashing smile, then as swiftly as she had run away before she disappeared from the Great Hall.

He stood staring after her, thinking that this at least was a diversion he had not expected, and certainly a very attractive one.

Chapter Three

The Duke was in the Picture Gallery, looking with pleasure at some of the very fine pictures collected by his ancestors.

He realised that what they had done which had been so intelligent, if perhaps unconsciously so, was to collect the leading contemporary artists of their own time.

He was especially admiring three very fine Van Dycks, several Gainsboroughs, and, obviously acquired by one discerning Minster, some excellent Dutch and French pictures all of the same period.

There was not a great number of them, but they were all, the Duke thought, pictures which he was proud to own and which he felt he had been remiss in not admiring more frequently.

He was standing in front of a Van Dyck to which he knew he bore a resemblance when he heard soft footsteps coming down the uncarpeted floor of the Gallery and saw Fabia coming towards him.

As she reached his side she looked up at him and he saw that her strange green-gold eyes were worried, and there was also, he thought, a look of pleading in them.

"What is it?" he asked.

"I . . . I have something to say to Your Grace," she said, "and I am . . . afraid it may make you angry."

The Duke smiled.

"I cannot imagine anything at the moment that

would make me angry, but I will certainly listen to what you have to say."

She clasped her hands together like a child who was giving herself courage and said:

"I have just been . . . told that you have . . . brought your . . . Chef with . . . you."

The Duke realised that this was Mr. Garston's doing and that one of his junior-Chefs must have been travelling in the brake with the other servants who had weighed it down as they left London.

"I am very particular about my food," he answered, "and if I am to stay here for any length of time I shall require the dishes I enjoy when I am in any of my other houses."

"I was . . . afraid that was what you . . . would say," Fabia answered.

She sounded so upset about it that the Duke asked curiously:

"Why should it perturb you?"

"Can you not . . . understand," she answered, looking up at him again, "that all the staff here have been . . . longing and . . . praying for you to visit them? And have thought of . . . nothing but how to . . . please you when you did so?"

There was a note in her voice that made the Duke raise his eye-brows in surprise as she went on:

"Mrs. Godwin, who used to cook for your grandmother . . . you always called her 'Goody,' I believe . . . has related to me over and over again the special dishes you enjoyed and how she would invent some new ones especially to please you. I think if she is . . . turned out of her . . . kitchen it will . . . break her heart."

There was no doubt, the Duke realised, that it would also upset Fabia.

After only a slight pause he answered:

"If Mrs. Godwin is still here, then of course she must cook for me as she did in the past!"

Fabia gave a little cry of sheer delight.

"Do you mean that? Do you . . . really mean it?"

"Will you go and tell Mrs. Godwin I am looking forward to my dinner tonight, and ask Barker to send the senior servant who came down from London to speak to me?"

"I will tell him at once!" Fabia cried. "And you will make Mrs. Godwin so very happy! Thank you!"

She sped away in her usual swift, graceful manner, and the Duke found himself smiling at the way his visit was progressing in a very different manner from what he had expected.

From long experience he knew that the older servants he employed either at Minster or at any of his other houses thought they had a proprietory claim, and there was no doubt that Garston had made a mistake in supplementing the staff that was already at Queen's Hoo.

The Duke supposed it was because he had not visited the house for so long that no-one had any idea of how many of the original servants were left.

Thinking back now, he recalled Mrs. Godwin as being a large, cheerful woman who made ginger-bread snaps for his tea and highly decorated birthday and Christmas cakes.

She also provided him with special treats in the holidays whether they were ordered by his grandmother or not.

'I must go and talk to her later,' the Duke thought as he saw one of the servants from London, his under-Butler, advancing towards him.

He knew that Barker would already be resenting his arrival and this would be another bone of contention.

When the man reached him the Duke gave him instructions that all the servants who had come down from London were to return the next day.

In the meantime they were not to interfere in any way with the running of the household at Queen's Hoo, nor were they to wait on him personally.

As he was speaking he thought that Fabia would be pleased, and he was not surprised when as soon as he was alone again she came to find him in the Library and said in a voice that seemed to lilt with happiness:

"Thank you! Thank you! You have made everybody here so very happy, and Mrs. Godwin is cooking you a feast for dinner! You will find it is a marathon of a meal."

The Duke laughed.

"Then I expect you to help me eat it."

There was a little pause before Fabia asked:

"Is Your Grace... intending that I shall... dine with you?"

"Of course!" he replied. "You cannot expect me to endure the marathon all by myself."

"Hannah said you would not... want me and... anyway it would be... incorrect."

"I think it would be far more incorrect for you, as my guest, to leave me to eat alone. Or, looking at it from another aspect, as you are more at home here than I am, it would be extremely incorrect for you not to be hospitable towards me!"

Fabia gave a little laugh.

"I doubt if Hannah would follow the logic of that answer! But please, I would like very much to dine with Your Grace, if you will not find it a bore."

"I insist that you do so," the Duke said firmly. "After all, I need you to tell me about my house and the way I should behave in it."

"You are teasing me... at least I hope so!" Fabia said in a low voice. "And it was... perhaps very... impertinent of me to... interfere."

"No, you were absolutely right," the Duke replied, "and it was something I should have thought of myself if it had not been such a very long time since I have visited Queen's Hoo."

"Far too long!" Fabia said. "Every year Barker and the other old servants used to say: 'Perhaps His Grace'll come in the spring.' 'Perhaps His Grace'll come in the autumn.' They were always disappointed."

"Now you are definitely making me feel uncomfortable," the Duke said. "So instead, let us talk about you."

"There are so many things I would rather hear about Your Grace," Fabia replied quickly.

The Duke thought that most women would be only too willing to talk about themselves, and he knew that there was in fact a great deal he wished to learn about Fabia.

Instead for the moment he found himself listening to what she told him about the house, of the bad winter when part of the roof fell in, and of another year when the gales brought down some of the finest trees.

She also made him laugh over the terrible commotion there had been when it was discovered that mice had nibbled away some of the embroidery of the bed in which Queen Elizabeth herself had slept.

"Mrs. Feather, who you will remember is the Housekeeper," Fabia said, "was in tears, and two of the housemaids were dismissed because they should have noticed it sooner."

"Dismissed?" the Duke questioned. "I suspect as they were probably local girls that was a very harsh punishment."

Fabia smiled.

"Because they were so upset, their sentence was reduced to being sent back to the village for three weeks without any wages."

"I can see this house is run in a very autocratic manner," the Duke said.

Fabia shook her head.

"No, everything is done to keep it in perfect condition for you."

The Duke could not find an answer to this, and they talked about the garden until it was time to go dress for dinner.

When he came downstairs again to the Great Hall where Barker was waiting with a bottle of champagne which had been well chilled, he thought the house looked even more magnificent in candlelight than it had when he had first arrived.

Outside, the sun was sinking in a blaze of glory and the first stars were twinkling in the sky.

When the Duke had looked out his bedroom window at the mist rising over the stream and the shadows purple beneath the trees, he had thought there was a mystery about Queen's Hoo that he had not found in any of his other properties.

The Hall was filled with the fragrance of flowers, and the Duke was aware that in his evening-clothes with his white shirt and tail-coat he fitted in with the elegance and atmosphere as if in fact he were one of his own ancestors.

"Because tonight is a special night," he said when he held a glass of champagne in his hand, "I must drink a toast to Her Majesty and thank her, as my grandmother used to do, for having commanded this house to be built for her."

"This is a happy day for all of us, Your Grace," Barker answered.

And the Duke thought once again how much Queen's Hoo meant to the people who lived in it.

Then Fabia came in through the door which led into the outer Hall, in which there was a carved oak staircase, and the Duke thought she might have stepped out of one of the pictures he had been admiring in the Gallery.

She was wearing a white gown with a full skirt and a lace bertha which was off her shoulders in the fashion set by Queen Victoria. Her hair was parted in the middle with soft curls on either side of her small face.

Because she was excited, her eyes seemed enormous, and the Duke, as an expert in a woman's appearance, realised that to celebrate his home-coming and also to be decorative Fabia had fashioned for herself a small wreath of fresh flowers which she wore at the back of her head.

There were two blossoms in the front of her bodice, and she looked very young and very spring-like as she came out of the shadows into the light from the candles.

She seemed to float towards the Duke before she curtseyed to him, and when she raised her head he thought the light in her eyes seemed to come from within her.

"Good-evening, Fabia!" he said. "I was just saying to Barker that we must drink a toast to the Queen."

"Yes, of course, we must do that!" Fabia agreed in a rapt little voice which told the Duke that she was not only very excited but was also admiring his appearance.

He was used to women looking at him with admiration, but he thought the expression in Fabia's eyes was different in a way he could not exactly explain.

Barker handed Fabia a glass of champagne, and the Duke asked:

"Shall I make the toast, Fabia, or will you?"

"You, of course!"

"Very well," he agreed, and raising his glass to the picture he said:

"To Your Majesty, who loved England, and I think too must have loved Queen's Hoo as we Minsters have done in the past and will continue to do in the centuries to come!"

He emptied the champagne in his glass and realised that Fabia had sipped hers before she said:

"That was lovely! A beautiful, beautiful toast which I shall always remember."

When they went in to dinner the Duke found that the Dining-Room, which he remembered as a particularly fine room, was also decorated with flowers.

Barker had brought out the best silver from the safe, and there was a huge Galleon with wind-filled sails

in the centre of the table and the bases of the candela-
bra were wreathed with flowers.

There were various goblets and comfit dishes which
the Duke remembered from the past.

He was aware without being told that although
there had been nobody to admire them, Barker had
kept them polished and ready for use for just such an
occasion as this all the years he had been absent.

Fabia had been right in saying that Mrs. Godwin
would provide a magnificent feast.

As course succeeded course, the Duke was aware
that every dish he had ever enjoyed as a boy and a
young man had been included on the menu.

While they were different from those he liked in
London, he knew that what he was eating was the best
English cooking it was possible to obtain.

Because it was fashionable to employ only French
Chefs, he had grown used to rich sauces with almost
every dish.

Now he found it was quite a welcome change to
taste food with its natural flavour unobscured.

Noticing as he ate that Fabia was watching him
anxiously to see what he liked and disliked, he thought
again that she might be the hostess and he the guest,
and he was amused to see how Queen's Hoo had
become so peculiarly her own and meant so much to
her personally.

'One day,' he thought to himself, 'she will marry.
Then she will find it hard to feel the same about her
husband's house. Perhaps it is a mistake for her to
become so involved with what after all is not really her
home.'

He was about to say something to that effect when
Fabia continued to tell him what had happened during
his absence and to speak of the treasures of the house as
if she loved each one.

When the meal was finished and the servants had
withdrawn, the Duke sat back comfortably in a high-

"Come, enter my world of love..."

Barbara Cartland

Receive absolutely free your choice of any four of these bestselling romances as your introduction to an exciting new reader's service.

13984	13942	14360	13985
14361	14504	14503	14996
20117	20112	13647	14833

Fall in love 18 times a year with...

The Barbara Cartland Romance Program

 **Charter Subscription Offer**

Now there's a special new way to enter Barbara Cartland's world of love. You can become a charter subscriber to The Barbara Cartland Romance Program. You'll enjoy substantial cash savings and time-saving convenience. And you'll be assured of receiving every thrilling new book by the Queen of Romance.

As a charter subscriber, choose *any four titles* on the reverse side *absolutely free.* Then each month in the Program you'll receive one or two new Barbara Cartland romances. Over the course of a year, 18 magical romances will be sent directly to your home. Each will be a brand-new, full-length, original novel. And in every one you'll share special moments in romantic rendezvous between captivating heroines and dashing heroes—as you bask in the elegance of crystal chandeliers and the glittering ballrooms of 19th century high society.

By dealing directly with the publisher, you'll enjoy many advantages:
• A *substantial savings* off the cover prices
• *No* shipping or handling charges
• The *convenience* of home delivery
• *Special discounts* on Bantam Books' large selection of titles

 **Satisfaction Guaranteed**

If, at any time, you're not completely delighted, you may cancel and receive a full refund of the unused portion of your subscription fee.

So act now to have the latest Barbara Cartland titles delivered to your door. Mark your choice of four free books on the Reservation Certificate and mail it today. Then we'll rush you your four books and make sure you receive next month's exciting shipment.

Reservation Certificate

Yes! Please begin my subscription to The Barbara Cartland Romance Program and send me the four free books I have specified. I understand that there are no shipping or handling charges. If at any time I am not completely delighted, I may cancel and you'll refund the undelivered portion of my subscription.

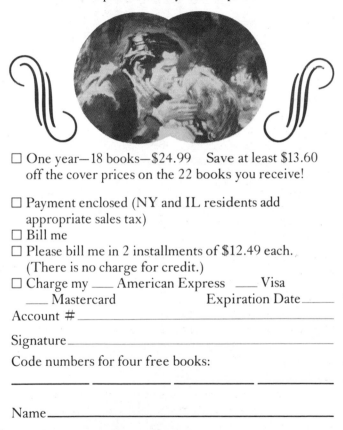

☐ One year—18 books—$24.99   Save at least $13.60 off the cover prices on the 22 books you receive!

☐ Payment enclosed (NY and IL residents add appropriate sales tax)

☐ Bill me

☐ Please bill me in 2 installments of $12.49 each. (There is no charge for credit.)

☐ Charge my ___ American Express ___ Visa
    ___ Mastercard   Expiration Date____

Account # _____

Signature _____

Code numbers for four free books:

_____ _____ _____ _____

Name _____

Address _____

City _____ State _____ Zip _____

This charter subscription good in U.S. only and for a limited time.   B

BUSINESS REPLY MAIL

FIRST CLASS   PERMIT NO. **28**   NORWOOD, NJ

POSTAGE WILL BE PAID BY ADDRESSEE

The Barbara Cartland Romance Program

Bantam Books
P.O. Box 224
Norwood, N.J. 07648

GK

backed armchair to sip a glass of the most excellent brandy which had been in the cellar since the end of the last century.

He looked at Fabia sitting beside him and thought almost with surprise how quickly the time had passed since they had sat down to dinner.

He had enjoyed every moment and had not, as he had expected, been in the least bored.

"Surely you find it very lonely here," he asked aloud, "with no companions of your own age? Or perhaps you have friends who visit you?"

"I am not . . . alone," Fabia replied.

"Then you have friends locally," he said. "Tell me their names. I may remember them."

"There is nobody in the neighbourhood who comes here."

"And yet you say you are not alone?"

It struck him once again that there was somebody perhaps on the Estate with whom she thought herself to be in love.

It was difficult to think that any woman could seem so happy unless there was a reason for it; and the reason, the Duke thought cynically, invariably was a man.

"It is not . . . like that," Fabia said almost as if she could read his thoughts.

"Then what is it like?"

He was sure she was being evasive.

At the same time, because the food had been good and the wine excellent and he had found himself interested and amused by what Fabia had told him, he was in a mellow mood.

"Now is the time for you to tell me about yourself," he said when she did not speak, "and, may I add, I insist upon knowing all about you."

He paused before he added:

"Otherwise I shall be quite certain that my 'Sleeping Beauty' is in fact a figment of my imagination and you will vanish as I expected you to do after I had first seen you."

As he spoke he remembered something else and went on:

"I would also like you to explain to me why when you first opened your eyes you said that you were dreaming of me, and then strangely enough you did not recognise who I was."

There was silence, until without looking at him Fabia said:

"If I tried to... explain... I think it would be... difficult for... you to understand."

The Duke raised his eye-brows.

"Are you suggesting that I am too stupid, too obtuse, or perhaps that what you have to say will shock me?"

Because he was still thinking there must be a man involved somewhere, there was undoubtedly a mocking note in his voice which Fabia did not miss.

There was a definite pause and he added:

"Perhaps you thought at first I was somebody else, and as I am curious I must insist that you answer my first question."

Fabia thought for a moment. Then she said:

"Do you remember... hearing about your ancestor Lord Prothero Minster?"

The Duke wondered what this could have to do with that he wished to hear before he replied:

"I seem to know the name."

"There is a portrait of him at the top of the staircase."

"Of course! Now I remember!" the Duke said. "I believe he was a strange man who studied astrology and made some weird pronouncements which encouraged people to think that he was mad."

"He was not mad," Fabia answered. "He was merely very much in advance of his time."

"I think I am right in saying that when my

great-great-great uncle," the Duke said, "for that is
what he was, was alive George II was on the throne."

"You are right," Fabia said, "and your grandmother
told me about him and allowed me to read his diaries."

The Duke looked surprised.

"His diaries? I had no idea he kept any."

"They are very precious and are locked up in the
Library."

"But you were allowed to read them?"

"Yes. I found them fascinating and they helped me
to understand Queen's Hoo."

"In what way?"

Again she was silent, and as the Duke watched her
exquisite little profile as she looked away from him he
wondered what she was hiding.

"I am waiting to hear," he said, "what Uncle
Prothero has to do with your saying you are not alone
here."

"Before I tell you that," Fabia replied, "you should
really read his diaries yourself. But I will try to explain
a little . . . of what he . . . believed."

The Duke looked puzzled.

He thought the conversation was unusual and only
hoped he would not have to listen to some boring
treatise by a relation long since dead.

"Your Uncle Prothero," Fabia began, "believed
that the world is encircled by waves of vibrations which
eternally revolve, retaining everything that happens on
the earth and perhaps on other planets as well."

She glanced quickly to see if the Duke was listening
and went on:

"He was sure that one day we would be able to tap
these waves and hear not only things that happened
thousands of years ago but also what is happening in the
time in which we live."

The Duke looked even more puzzled.

"I am trying to follow this," he said, "but it is a
little obscure."

"I thought it was, at first," Fabia agreed, "but can you not understand the possibility that while we are talking to each other, everything we are saying is being carried away on vibrating waves, and if somebody in another part of the world is receptive to them they might be able to listen to us!"

"What an extraordinary idea!" the Duke exclaimed.

"But an exciting one!" Fabia said. "And your ancestor went further than that."

"I cannot imagine how," the Duke said a little sceptically.

"He thought that one day in the far-off future, people would even be able to see what had happened in the past and watch the murder of Julius Caesar or admire the beauty of Cleopatra. Even more exciting, we could watch as it was happening the Queen and the Prince Consort eating their dinner in Buckingham Palace!"

The Duke laughed.

"I cannot imagine anything more embarrassing than never to know who might be peeping in on us!"

"Lord Prothero thought we would have to use an instrument of some sort, which he guessed would be something like the telescope with which he viewed the stars."

"When that happens, I hope I am not alive to see it," the Duke said. "But as it is certainly not happening at the moment, I still cannot understand how my ancestor's strange prognostications can have saved you from feeling lonely."

Fabia hesitated before she replied, and he knew she was choosing her words with care.

"Long before I read Lord Prothero's idea of vibrations encircling the world in waves," she said at length, "I was aware of the . . . vibrations . . . within this . . . house."

"In what way?"

"I think at first," Fabia said, "it was after . . . your grandmother died."

She looked at the Duke a little apprehensively as she said quietly:

"Although the Duchess's body lay in the family vault, I was aware that she was still here."

The Duke stiffened.

"You thought you saw her ghost?"

Fabia shook her head.

"No, no, not her ghost, but her spirit was here in the house she had loved and which she did not wish to leave."

It flashed through the Duke's mind that it was wrong and perhaps unhealthy for a young girl to be preoccupied with death or with the idea of survival after death.

He had always believed that ghosts were a lot of nonsense and that people who thought they saw them had either an overactive imagination or in many cases had imbibed too freely.

He was aware that Fabia was looking at him as if she expected him either to mock at her or to tell her not to be foolish. Instead he said quietly:

"I think you must explain a little more fully."

"You are . . . really . . . interested?"

"I promise you that what you are saying interests me enormously," the Duke answered. "I am trying to follow what you have reasoned out for yourself, but I am finding it a little difficult."

"I can understand that, because it is so long since you have lived in Queen's Hoo," Fabia said. "Now that you have come back, I expect the house will explain itself to you as it did to me."

"What did it explain?"

"When I first came here," Fabia said simply, "I was aware of . . . you."

"Of me?" the Duke asked in surprise. "I suppose you mean that my grandmother talked of me."

She shook her head.

"No, I was aware of you as a little boy. I could not

see you, but I could feel you and at times I could hear your voice in the places where you had played . . . the woods and of course the Temple."

"You knew this without anybody telling you?" the Duke asked.

Fabia nodded.

"I could feel you so vividly that it was almost as if you were beside me. It was then, after I had read what Lord Prothero had written, that I understood."

"You understood what?"

"Vibrations we give out from ourselves, if we are strong enough, can remain on the atmosphere or in a place, so that they can be picked up, just as Lord Prothero thought that one day we could pick them up with a machine."

"You think everybody can do such things?"

"No, I think most people do not have the time, or are seldom alone, or perhaps are just not interested."

"Or are not so perceptive," the Duke added.

"I like to think I am that," Fabia said. "I also think that as a boy you gave out particularly strong vibrations. They have therefore impressed themselves on the atmosphere, and it was easy for me to pick them up."

"And do I emit those vibrations now?" the Duke asked.

To his surprise Fabia did not answer, and after a moment he enquired, an incredulous note in his voice:

"Are you saying I have lost them?"

"Not . . . exactly . . . or perhaps I should say not . . . completely."

"But you do not feel them?"

She shook her head and it struck the Duke that it was not particularly complimentary.

As if Fabia had thought the same thing she said:

"It is quite understandable. When you were here as a young boy and Queen's Hoo meant so much to you, there was the wonder, the joy, and the excitement of it. Everything that you felt and thought, in fact your whole self, was concentrated in one place, and your sheer joy of living was very, very strong."

"And that is something I have now lost?" the Duke asked as if he could not believe such a thing could happen.

"It is ... perhaps a little ... dispersed," Fabia said uncomfortably.

"I cannot understand why," the Duke remarked. "You say that when you were dreaming of me it was of my past vibrations. Yet when you woke up completely you did not recognise me as the same person."

Fabia did not answer but he knew she was looking unhappy.

"Tell me if that is the truth," he insisted. "I want to know."

She turned towards him and stretched out her arm across the table as she said:

"Please give me your hand."

The Duke put his hand on hers as she placed it palm upwards.

He thought as he did so that this was the strangest conversation he had ever had in his whole life, and undoubtedly it was a somewhat deflating one.

He was so used to every woman with whom he dined being flirtatious and looking at him with a very human, passionate invitation in her eyes that he was finding it difficult to adjust himself to what he was aware was the very impersonal attitude of his companion.

Then as Fabia's fingers closed over his he looked at her face, expecting to see a beguiling expression in her eyes and perhaps the soft parting of her lips.

But, to his surprise, Fabia's lashes were dark against her cheeks and her eyes were closed.

She held herself very still and was silent until at last she said:

"The vibrations are still there. I can feel them. They are a little indistinct and very different from what they were before."

"You mean when I was a boy?"

"When you were very young, and I think they were still being imprinted on the atmosphere at the time of your grandmother's death, but I cannot be sure."

She took her hand from his and went on:

"They will come back! To lose them would be very sad."

"For me?" the Duke enquired.

"Of course, because you would not be a vital part of the Universe, our earth, the flowers, the trees, the stars, the moon, and the sun. And whether we are receptive or weak depends on what we give into the atmosphere."

"Is this your theory or my ancestor's?" the Duke enquired.

"I think we all have to discover what we think and what we believe for ourselves," Fabia replied. "But it has certainly helped me to find that what I had been feeling was already written down in your uncle's diaries."

"What else did you feel besides my vibrations?" the Duke asked.

"Naturally in a house that has existed as long as Queen's Hoo the vibrations of the people who have lived here are still to be found in every room, and perhaps especially in the Hall."

"Why the Hall?"

"Because it has always been the centre of family life, where they gathered, where they talked, where decisions were made, and where sometimes there were tragedies."

"What sort of tragedies?"

"One man was murdered, and a duel was once fought in the Hall," Fabia replied. "The loser who was killed was the secret lover of the daughter of the house, and when he died she mourned him until she too died and they were together."

Fabia spoke in a very quiet tone of voice, as if she was following the story in her own mind.

Because the Duke felt he was being mesmerised by what she said, he asked almost sharply:

"I suppose that is what you have read in some book!"

"No," Fabia answered. "It has never been written down!"

"Then how do you know it is true?"

She looked at him and after a moment he said:

"Are you telling me that you could see it happen?"

She nodded and said:

"Just once I saw it. It must have been the anniversary of the day it occurred and the atmospherics were right.

"Then what you are saying," the Duke said, "is that actual past events can sometimes appear like pictures in front of us."

"Yes indeed," Fabia replied. "I have read in books about people seeing battles of long ago taking place, or where in a great Castle in Scotland people staying the night have seen a King murdered in their room and were told in the morning it was only a ghost."

"What you are saying," the Duke said slowly, as if he was trying to work it out for himself, "is that it was not a ghost but the actual scene being re-enacted in another century, because the vibrations which are revolving round the world all the time had just come to that particular spot at an opportune moment!"

Fabia clapped her hands together in an instinctive gesture of joy.

"You do understand!" she cried. "I never thought you would."

"I am trying to," the Duke said, "and I consider it an insult that you doubted me."

"I am sorry," she said quickly. "It was only that when I awoke and did not recognise you as the little boy of whom I was dreaming, I thought you were a

very handsome man but I did not feel your vibrations
reaching out towards mine."

"Is that something you often feel?"

"Not very often," she replied, "but when your
grandmother died they were there almost like a strong
light, which is why I know she is still here in the house,
although I am not always aware of her."

"And when you are?"

"I feel she is telling me that she is glad I am here
because I understand."

The Duke took a sip of his brandy, thinking that if
Eddie or his other friends heard what Fabia was saying
they would simply scoff at it.

It was incredible, although it seemed to him to
have a great deal of plausibility about it.

Yet in a way he was certain that he would find it far
harder to believe if he were not at Queen's Hoo.

As he listened to Fabia he could understand exactly what she meant by vibrations coming from his grandmother.

It was something he had felt himself, but he had
thought after she was dead that it was merely because
he had loved her so deeply and she had meant so much
in his life at a time when he was not happy at
home.

But he had not worked it out for himself.

Now he realised how she had shone in the Social
World in which she lived, how intelligent men of every
nationality gravitated towards her, and how Queen's
Hoo had always been an indivisible part of her.

It was somewhat humiliating to think he had not
realised it until this moment; that it had taken a young
girl to show him what he should have known and to
point out the shortcomings in himself.

Because he had not spoken for some minutes,
Fabia said a little nervously:

"I am sorry if you . . . feel I have been . . . rude
about Your Grace. I admire you very much, and I think

you look magnificent and exactly as you should do, but I could not help telling you . . . the truth."

"I am glad you did," the Duke replied, "although I admit to being somewhat surprised."

"Some people have no vibrations at all," Fabia said, "or they are so indecisive that they die and disappear into the Life Force and are never seen again."

"The Life Force?" the Duke questioned.

"This again was one of your ancestor's theories, that the Life Force grows stronger and stronger as more people are born, but only those who become intellectually and spiritually great in themselves survive individually after the death of the body."

"I have never thought of it before," the Duke said, "but it sounds to me entirely feasible."

"The rest are like the leaves on the trees, the grass in the fields, and the flowers in the gardens. When they die, the life in them goes back into the great Power House from which everybody draws their very existence—human beings, animals, nature itself. But some who are stronger than others live on as themselves."

"Do you think that is what you will do?" the Duke asked.

"I do not aspire to anything so exalted at the moment," she answered, "but I feel perhaps I have passed through many lives already to get as far as I have."

She smiled before she added:

"I am certain of only one thing: if I die at Queen's Hoo, I shall not be alone any more than I am alone here now. My vibrations will join with those who are here because it is the place where they were happy."

This was a thought that had never occurred to the Duke before, and when they left the Dining-Room, after talking for a very long time, he went to one of the windows in the Great Hall to pull back the velvet curtains and look out into the night.

By now the heavens were filled with stars and there was a young moon rising over the trees.

There was the light from the sky to lend an air of mystery to everything and to turn the stream into a ribbon of silver.

The Duke stood still as he looked and Fabia stood beside him. He thought it was typical that she did not speak but let the night speak for her, almost carrying on the conversation where she had left off.

Any other woman would have been chattering away and of course putting everything they said to each other onto a personal basis, so that it would be difficult to think of anything except that he was a man and she was a woman.

He had the feeling that although she was standing beside him, Fabia as she looked up at the stars had forgotten his existence.

Because it piqued him that she should be so impersonal, he said almost as if he challenged her:

> *"'She walks in beauty like the night*
> *In cloudless climes and starless skies*
> *And all that's best of dark and bright*
> *Meet in the aspect of her eyes.'"*

It was something he had said a dozen times to different women who in turn had told him either with their lips or with their eyes that as long as he thought them beautiful, nothing else mattered.

Fabia, however, did not even turn her face towards him, but merely said:

"I was thinking that Shelley would be more appropriate to what we have been saying."

"What particular lines?" the Duke asked.

> *"'Dust to the dust! but the pure spirit shall flow*
> *Back to the burning fountain whence it came,*
> *A portion of the eternal.'"*

This was so apt that the Duke found it annoying that he had not thought of it himself.

But Fabia was still looking at the stars and he felt incredibly that once again she had forgotten him.

Chapter Four

The Duke did not sleep for a long time as he was thinking over what Fabia had said at dinner.

Then he woke early, and deciding that he would ride sooner than his servants expected, he dressed and went to the stables.

He thought as he walked there that while he was at Queen's Hoo he would try out a number of his other horses besides Perseus, which was his favourite.

However, this morning he decided that Perseus would suit him better than any other mount, and as soon as he appeared in the stable-yard the grooms hurried to saddle the stallion.

"Good-marnin', Y'Grace!" said the old groom who had known him as a boy. "Oi were a-wishin' ter ask ye if Y'Grace would send ter Minster fer some more 'orses. Y'Grace'd want to try these out fer yerself afore they're ready fer visitors."

"I will think about it," the Duke said, knowing that he had no wish for those in the stables at Minster to know where he was.

"There's one person 'ere as'll be able to 'elp Y'Grace to break in 'em as is obstreperous," the groom went on.

The Duke at once guessed the answer, but he waited until the man added:

"Miss Wilton be the finest rider Oi've ever known fer a lady."

The Duke did not reply, but he thought to himself that it was what he might have expected.

Although she had an ethereal, fairy-like appearance, he had somehow been sure that Fabia would have an affinity with animals, which was a quality nearly always lacking in the beauties he pursued in London.

As Perseus came from the stable, rearing and bucking to show his independence, the Duke asked:

"Will Miss Wilton be riding this morning?"

"'Er's bin gone some time, Y'Grace," the groom replied. "'Er's always early. 'Er often catches the lads as work 'ere napping!"

The old groom laughed before he added:

"An' that's somethin' Y'Grace used ter do, an', if we wasn't about, saddle yer 'orse yerself!"

The Duke smiled, remembering that this was true and that he had often crept down to the stables particularly early in order to escape his Tutors who wanted him to pore over mathematics or Greek before breakfast.

He mounted Perseus, who immediately, feeling the master hand on the reins, settled down and behaved with propriety.

But the horse was fresh and the Duke knew a gallop would do him good.

He was wondering where Fabia would have gone, then knew instinctively that she would have ridden as he always had across the Park, being careful of rabbit-holes, then through the small wood at the end of it to what was always known as "The Long Mile."

It was a flat piece of ground with woods on either side of it.

The Duke had not only galloped there alone, but when he had his friends to stay from Eton, or later from Oxford, he had raced them from one end to the other and, he thought with satisfaction, had invariably been the winner.

He checked Perseus, who wanted to stretch his legs as they rode through the Park, then as they emerged from the wood which the Duke noted had grown thicker since he was last at Queen's Hoo, he saw

The Long Mile and in the distance the person he sought.

Fabia was just turning her horse and the Duke waited as she let him have his head and started back at a rate that increased step by step until she passed him with what he thought was the speed of lightning.

He was right in thinking she could ride. He knew by the way she held herself and her grace in the saddle that she was in fact exceptional.

She went by so quickly that he was not sure whether she had seen him or not.

Pressing his high hat firmly on his head, he set off after her, knowing as he did so that Perseus was determined to pass any other horse in any contest, for he enjoyed them just as much as his master did.

The Long Mile was by any accurate measure nearly two, and it took him some time before the Duke drew level with Fabia.

As he did so she flashed him a little smile and there was a mischievous look in her strange eyes, as if she realised he was trying to pass her to show his supremacy not only on a horse but also in other fields.

Then they were racing each other, the Duke determined to win because it was something he always did, although at this particular moment he was not absolutely certain that he could do so.

In fact they were still neck-and-neck when the end of the course was in sight and they were obliged to rein in their horses.

They both came to a standstill and even the Duke's voice was a little breathless as he said:

"I imagine without a Referee that was a dead heat."

Fabia smiled.

"I am of course prepared to concede victory to Your Grace if you insist upon it."

"Why should you do that?"

"Sprite and I are very grateful for the hospitality of your stables."

The Duke looked at the horse Fabia was riding and

realised it was a fine Thoroughbred but was not one of his.

He always kept horses in his different houses in case he should require them, but he could not remember Mr. Garston telling him that he was buying or sending any horses to Queen's Hoo.

He therefore suspected that the only horses he would find there were those that were necessary for his Agent to ride or to fetch and carry for the household.

"So Sprite is your horse," he said.

"The only valuable possession I own," Fabia answered, "and one of the things that worried me most, if you had turned us out last night, was what I could have done with Sprite."

The Duke smiled.

"You do not think he would have enjoyed sleeping in a hay-stack?"

"He would not have minded as long as I was there," Fabia answered. "At the same time, I would have been more concerned about him than myself."

The Duke thought that was what he might have expected her to feel, and he looked at her, thinking how elegant she looked on a horse that was jet black except for a star on its forehead and one white fetlock.

"I have a feeling," he said, "that Sprite obeys you as Perseus obeys me."

"Sprite will do anything I ask of him," Fabia replied, "and perhaps one day you would like to see a demonstration."

"I would enjoy that," the Duke answered, "but I think for the moment both Sprite and Perseus should get their breath."

"It is good for him to have someone to race," Fabia said.

"And for us," the Duke replied. "It has certainly swept away the cobwebs."

As he spoke he thought there were no cobwebs about Fabia.

There was a brightness and a kind of radiance

about her that he had never seen before in any woman so early in the morning.

It was not only that her eyes were unusual, but her hair was neatly bound with ribbons so that even the gallop had left her neat and tidy.

She was wearing a full riding-skirt of a dark green which was the colour of the fir trees, and instead of a jacket she wore a thin blouse of a pale green like the green of the young grass over which they were riding.

Fabia looked as if she were part of the countryside, and the sunshine on her very fair hair shone like the first fingers of dawn coming up the sky.

'She is lovely!' the Duke thought to himself. 'And if she was well dressed she would be a sensation in London!'

Then he thought that to take such a delicate flower to London and transplant her from Queen's Hoo might be a mistake.

Almost as if she was following his thoughts Fabia asked:

"How long is Your Grace intending to stay here?"

"I have not yet decided," the Duke replied. "I might move on to one of my other houses when Queen's Hoo ceases to amuse me."

"But surely you should be in London at this time of the year?" Fabia asked. "I always understood that the Season was very busy for those who move in the Social World and that there were Balls and Receptions every night."

"Would you enjoy the Social World?" the Duke asked.

Fabia laughed as she replied:

"No, indeed! I have no ambition to move in the circles my mother used to talk about, although if she had lived I know she would have wanted to present me to the Queen. But I doubt if we would ever have had enough money for our gowns, let alone the expense of renting a house in London."

"You would have enjoyed it if it had happened,"

the Duke insisted, almost as if he wanted her to admit that she had such ambitions.

"I cannot imagine anything more enjoyable or more wonderful than being here," Fabia said, "and I was thinking last night that I had not thanked you enough for understanding how in coming to live at Queen's Hoo I felt as if I had come home."

"How can you feel like that?" the Duke asked sharply. "Neither your father nor your mother are here with you, and despite what we talked about last night, I cannot believe that your 'vibrations,' as you call them, really compensate for human companionship and especially for admirers to tell you how lovely you look."

He spoke deliberately in a matter-of-fact way because he remembered what Fabia had told him last night. In fact, it was something that he was convinced he should not encourage in a young girl.

There was silence for a moment and he knew that Fabia was thinking over what he said, and because he felt he had perhaps been a little harsh and unfeeling he looked at her apprehensively.

Almost as if he willed her to do so, she turned her face towards him.

But far from looking worried or even insulted that he should disparage her feelings in such a way, he saw that her eyes were twinkling and there was, incredibly, an almost mocking smile on her lips.

"Now your mind is challenging your instinct," she said.

"Why do you say that?" the Duke asked.

"Because it is true," she answered. "You are trying to convince yourself in the daylight that what we talked about and what you admired last night was not true, was only a figment of my imagination."

Because this was so palpably the case, the Duke could not for a moment think of a suitable reply, and Fabia went on:

"There is no need for me to try to convince you.

Queen's Hoo will do that for you if you stay here long enough."

As she spoke she touched Sprite with her heel and was riding away, and it took the Duke a little time to catch up with her.

Breakfast was waiting for them when they returned to the house. The Breakfast-Room, which his grandmother had always used until she was very old because she thought it a weakness to breakfast in bed, looked out over the Rose Garden and caught the morning sun.

As the Duke looked in the silver dishes on the sideboard, each with a lighted candle beneath it to keep its contents warm, and on the table a large square of comb-honey and a bowl of fruit from the garden, he was once again stepping back in time.

It was the way he and his grandmother had always breakfasted, and they waited on themselves because the Duchess had said she disliked having to talk even to the servants first thing in the morning when she wished to compose her thoughts for the day.

This was something that Fabia was unlikely to have known, but the Duke realised that she was silent unless he spoke to her.

They sat in the sunshine, eating eggs, fresh mushrooms, and ham, all of which came from the Home Farm.

For the Duke there were devilled chicken-eggs, a favourite dish from the old days, which even the best of his chefs had never prepared as well as Mrs. Godwin.

He was hungry with an appetite he seldom had in London, and as he finished his second helping of devilled eggs he said:

"If I stay here long I shall grow so fat that I shall need a heavier horse than Perseus to carry me!"

"I think that is unlikely," Fabia replied, "and I expect you could still get into the clothes that you used to wear when you came here in the past."

The Duke looked at her questioningly.

"Are you telling me that my old clothes are still here?"

"Of course," she replied. "They have been treasured like everything else about you."

"You are frightening me," the Duke said. "I am beginning to think Queen's Hoo is a shrine—a kind of memorial—and if I am here long I shall be looking back into the past instead of forward to the future."

"That is where you are wrong," Fabia answered. "I believe that Queen's Hoo not only inspires those who live here but also enlarges and develops their facility for living."

"How can you possibly believe that?" the Duke asked. "Living here alone, how can you have any idea of the effect the house could have on other people apart from a lot of elderly servants?"

He spoke in a manner which he told himself was sheer common sense, and he was sure it was a mistake to encourage Fabia in her dreams, which were frankly just moonshine.

"I can see," she said after a moment, "that when you were here you were not a great reader."

"What do you mean by that?"

"You will find in the Library one bookcase which is filled with the history of the Minsters," she said. "I have placed them all together, starting with your ancestor who built the house and ending with your grandmother's diaries, which she kept every day of her life."

"I knew that she always kept a diary," the Duke said slowly, "But I did not realise, although I suppose I never thought about it, that they contained anything interesting."

"They are such a fascinating account of her life and times that I am sure they should be published."

"Published?" the Duke exclaimed.

"Yes, why not? You were so lucky to have known Her Grace for so long," Fabia went on. "She was not only very intelligent but a wise and astute judge of character."

"I certainly knew that," the Duke agreed.

"She wrote down all that she thought and felt about the great and famous people who came to the house in London, to Minster, and of course here. It is absolutely fascinating what she says about them, and I am quite certain it is of great historical interest."

"Then I must certainly read them," the Duke said, "But that does not really answer my question."

"Quite a number of your ancestors wrote very eloquently about either themselves or previous members of the family," Fabia said, "and there is a common denominator about those who lived here which if you follow it down the centuries is very revealing."

"In what way?" the Duke asked.

"They all gradually became convinced that they had a duty to contribute something important to the future of the country."

The Duke stared at her. Then he said:

"Are you trying to convince me that that was the influence of the house itself?"

"It is very obvious to me that the inspiration came from here and that each succeeding generation thought the same, felt the same, and gradually translated their thoughts into deeds."

The Duke was silent. Then he said:

"I suppose that in a not very subtle manner you are preaching to me!"

Fabia smiled and for the first time he realised that when she did so there was a dimple in each cheek.

"I would not presume to do anything so impertinent, Your Grace," she answered, "but of course 'if the cap fits . . .'"

"You *are* being impertinent!" the Duke said half-seriously. "Queen's Hoo or no Queen's Hoo, I intend to carry on the finest traditions of the Minsters, but I do believe that anything I do will derive not from the house but from myself."

As he spoke he knew that despite his brave words he had in fact, since becoming the Duke, achieved little except in the sporting world, and his social reputation did not particularly embellish the family history in the way that Fabia was speaking of it.

Because the thought annoyed him, he rose from the table and said:

"If we are going to ride, since I wish to see what is happening on the Estate as a whole, then I think we should leave."

"Yes, of course," Fabia agreed. "But you are quite certain you want me to come with you and you would not rather go alone?"

"I have invited you to come," the Duke said, "but if you have other commitments . . ."

She laughed at him.

"They are not what you would consider particularly serious or important," she answered, "and because they are things rather than people, they will wait for me and not be annoyed at having to do so."

The Duke knew without being told that she was thinking that if he had not been there she would have gone to the Herb Garden or the Temple and not felt alone because of the vibrations she felt there.

He did not want to think about it but it persisted in his mind, and to rid himself of such ridiculous ideas he walked quickly from the Breakfast-Room, saying as he did so:

"I wish to leave in fifteen minutes."

Fabia was waiting for him in the Hall when exactly a quarter-of-an-hour later he came downstairs.

He saw at once that her concession to the importance of riding with him was to put on a hat.

His experienced eye told him it was by no means new, but the piece of gauze that encircled the crown and fell down behind was very becoming, and because it was green it added to his impression that she was part of the countryside.

Perseus and Sprite were waiting for them and the Duke deliberately had not suggested they be changed for two fresher horses, feeling sure that Fabia would rather ride Sprite than any other.

He had by now determined that he would need more horses and had already written a note to Mr. Garston, instructing him that horses should be sent to Queen's Hoo, but secretly, without there being any chance of his whereabouts becoming known.

He suggested that his hunters in Leicestershire should be brought to him immediately, and that the Manager of his stable in Newmarket should buy anything which was really good in the Sales.

He then ordered a groom to carry his instructions to London as quickly as possible and went to join Fabia.

He realised as he did so that he had committed himself to staying at Queen's Hoo for quite some time.

He knew already that this was what he wanted to do and there was no question at the moment of his leaving or moving elsewhere.

They rode first to the Home Farm, which was, the Duke saw at once, in model condition.

The farmer and his wife greeted him effusively and obviously were eager to talk of the old days. In fact he enjoyed sitting in their Parlour and sipping their home-made cider that had mellowed well in the cool of the cellars beneath the house.

He could also see that the cattle were fat, the calves were exceptionally strong, and the rest of the livestock might have stepped out of an idealised picture of rural England.

As they rode away he said to Fabia:

"I am surprised!"

"Why?" she asked.

"Because I always thought that when landlords were absent or what you would call neglectful of their Estates, things went wrong."

She did not reply and he went on:

"Do you realise that there were no complaints

from the farmer and I could certainly find no criticism to make."

She smiled with what he thought was delight and he said:

"Are you going to tell me that this is another proof of the magic of Queen's Hoo?"

"Of course it is!" she replied. "Your grandmother said it carried on the traditions not of your father, who never lived here, but of your grandfather who did for some part of every year and his father before him."

She glanced at the Duke under her eye-lashes as she went on:

"As I think I have already made you understand, although you are trying not to accept it, the vibrations in Queen's Hoo embrace not only the family of Minster but those who serve them."

"I refuse to believe it!" the Duke said firmly. "If the employees are happy at Minster, as they are, it is due to good organisation and good management."

"Of course," Fabia agreed, "but who does the organising?"

"The Manager!" the Duke answered.

"And who chooses the Manager?"

"The employer—myself!"

"And your grandmother chose the father of the present Agent here, who is called Fenton, so it all comes back to the same thing. It is the Minsters who create the right atmosphere and therefore own farms like the one we have just visited."

"It is too plausible and too easy," the Duke protested.

As he rode on, he thought that perhaps the next farm would be different. However, if it was not quite as picturesque, it was just as efficient and the people who worked there were just as delighted to see him.

As they rode home for luncheon the Duke was silent.

He was thinking it must be coincidence that everything here seemed to be in better order than on any of his other Estates.

Although the farms both at Minster and on his other properties were efficient, there was not the same atmosphere about them which he had found this morning.

He told himself, however, that he was not going to give in so easily and acknowledge that Fabia was right.

He was still convinced that what she was trying to persuade him into believing was just the enthusiasm of a young girl who had not enough practical things with which to occupy her mind and had therefore surrendered herself to the supernatural.

'Young women often take up religion or cults of some sort,' he thought, 'and when they fall in love they find a man far more satisfying.'

That explanation might be cynical, but he thought that was what one inevitably became as one grew older, and he was not going to be caught by this airy-fairy nonsense which was just a figment of Fabia's over-active mind.

At luncheon he deliberately talked of the amusements he found in London, the Theatres, the Opera, the pageantry at Buckingham Palace, and the social gatherings which took place every morning in Rotten Row.

"Sprite would be very much admired there," he said, "and so would you. You are wasted on an audience of birds and butterflies."

There was an expression in Fabia's strange eyes which told him that she was astute enough to realise why he was talking in such a way.

"I think, as you are a Minster," he said, "I should speak to some of our relations, make arrangements for you to meet the rest of the family, and next year to have a Season in London after you have been presented to the Queen."

Fabia looked at him curiously.

"Are you serious?" she asked.

"Quite serious!" the Duke replied. "I have only just thought of it, and of course it is right that as your cousin, even though a distant one, I should be responsible for you."

Fabia looked away from him across the room and he knew she was thinking.

It struck him that most young girls to whom he had made such an offer would have jumped over the moon with excitement at the chance of being to all intents and purposes his Ward and having their future assured through being under the protection of such an influential family.

But Fabia was silent for a long time until at length she said:

"I am wondering what is . . . right for me to . . . do."

"Right?" the Duke asked.

"I never imagined," she said, "that you or anybody else might suggest such a thing to me. Although I know it is something Mama would have liked, I am not certain that I should not stay here."

"Are you really saying," the Duke asked, "that you would rather stay here alone, as you have been doing until I arrive, than take your place as a member of the family in the Social World in which every door will be open to you?"

"But . . . if I do . . . that," Fabia said in a low voice, "what . . . happens next?"

"That is an easy question," the Duke replied. "You will meet some charming man who will want to marry you; he will ask my consent; and if I consider he is the right husband for you—and I shall be very particular that he is—you will be married and live happily ever afterwards."

He expected Fabia's eyes to light up with excitement at the idea, but instead there was a look of contemplation on her face and there was no sign of her smile and the dimples in her cheeks.

"What is wrong with that?" the Duke asked.

"I am . . . not certain," she replied. "I will . . . think about it in the Temple, where it is easier to think than anywhere else."

The Duke remembered that that was what he had thought as a boy, then thrust the thought away from him.

"I cannot see that the Temple has anything to do with it!" he said sharply. "And it is ridiculous to imagine that when I have left you can stay here alone with nobody to talk to except the servants."

He took a sip of wine before he added:

"Now that I have decided your future, we need not worry about it any more, except to choose which of my relatives I shall approach to act as your Chaperone."

"Please do not do . . . anything in a . . . hurry," Fabia said. "It is kind of you, very . . . very kind . . . but I have not yet . . . agreed to your . . . suggestion."

"I shall insist that you do so," the Duke retorted. "It is something which, if you like, you owe to your Minster blood."

"That is what I am telling myself," Fabia said in a low voice. "At the same time . . ."

"Oh, for goodness' sake!" the Duke interrupted. "You cannot be so stupid as not to see the advantages of what I have just offered you. There is no alternative, no question of 'yes' or 'no.' It is what you will do, because as head of the family I expect you to obey me."

Now there was a smile on Fabia's lips.

"You are being very authoritative," she said, "and perhaps that is a good sign."

"Are you saying I have ever been anything else?" the Duke enquired.

"I think you have doubtless been so in matters concerning yourself. But this is my decision, and I intend to make it for myself and not let anybody else overrule me."

"Now you are being provocative," the Duke said," "and do not forget that I can always have the last word."

"By throwing me out of Queen's Hoo?" Fabia flashed. "If you do that, after you have gone I might come back and live in the Temple and defy you to move me!"

The Duke felt that the conversation had reverted to the level of a fairy-story.

"I think you would find it cramped," he said, "if you stayed there long, and it would certainly be too small for Hannah and Sprite to stay with you."

"That is true," Fabia said, "but . . . please , . . . please do not let Hannah have any . . . idea of what you have . . . suggested for me until I have made up . . . my mind."

"What you are saying," the Duke said, "is that Hannah who has a great deal more common sense than you have, would certainly support me."

"But of course!" Fabia said. "Hannah loves me and she wanted me to live in the Social World which Mama and Papa could never afford."

The Duke did not reply and she went on:

"Servants are snobs, Mama always said that, and I am sure all the ones you employ not only love you as a man but are very proud and puffed up with their own consequence because you are a Duke."

The Duke laughed, knowing this was true. Then he said:

"I cannot promise, but to please Hannah I must obviously try to provide you with a Duke for a husband."

Fabia shook her head.

"I think it unlikely that I shall ever be married," she said quietly.

The Duke looked at her in astonishment.

"What an extraordinary statement!" he exclaimed. "Why should you say that?"

Fabia did not reply and after a moment he said:

"I want an answer to my question."

"You will disapprove of it if I tell you."

"That is something you have to risk," he said, "for as your Guardian, it is very important that I should know your feelings in this extremely important matter."

"Very well," Fabia said. "You will not agree with me . . . and you will think I am talking . . . nonsense . . . but

I am quite certain the only way I am to be happy is if the vibrations of my husband link with mine."

"So we are back to vibrations," the Duke said drily. "I really think that has very little to do with it."

"On the contrary," Fabia said, "they have everything. The strongest vibration in the world is love, and if we love someone we know immediately if they vibrate to us and we vibrate to them. There would be no question of our ever being bored with them or disagreeing on anything of real importance. In fact, we are linked together as one person and not two."

The Duke looked at her and it flashed through his mind that perhaps this was the reason why he had always become bored so quickly with women and found that after a short while they no longer interested him.

Then he told himself once again that this was a lot of rubbish and that people had been happily married since Adam and Eve without worrying about their vibrations.

"Your grandmother told me once, when I was looking at the portrait of your grandfather," Fabia was saying softly, "That when she saw him she knew he was the one man who would matter in her life, and in the same second of time he fell in love with her."

The Duke remembered hearing this before and he had thought it was just something that occurred to two people in a million and was very unlikely to happen to him.

"So what is called 'love at first sight,'" he said drily, "you attribute to these hypothetical waves going round and round the world."

"We also give them out ourselves to everybody with whom we come in contact, and the reason you were happy this morning was that the people we met liked and admired you. Their vibrations flashed from them to you, and you instantly felt happy and at ease with them."

"Surely that is a very different thing altogether?" the Duke asked.

"Not really," Fabia said. "Just as Perseus and Sprite pick up the vibrations of the people dealing with them and react to them, so we do the same with every person and every animal we meet."

The Duke did not say so aloud, but he thought that the reason why Perseus behaved so badly with the grooms who looked after him was that they were frightened of him, while Perseus acknowledged him as his master.

However, he wanted to challenge Fabia and he said:

"You are making life too simple, and when you have lived as long as I have in a world with people of very conflicting and diverse characters, you will realise it is difficult to find a universal or reasonable explanation for their behaviour."

Fabia did not argue with him. She merely said:

"Think of Queen's Hoo and tell me what is the first word that comes into your mind."

The Duke had a vision of what he had seen that morning when they had ridden through the wood.

In front of them Queen's Hoo was glowing in the sunlight, pink and warm as the skin of a peach, the white and red Royal standard was vivid against the blue of the sky, the windows glittered, and the stream beneath the house was a streak of gold.

"Beauty!" he replied.

"And the next word?"

The Duke was just about to say it, then prevented it from escaping his lips because it would be conceding too much to Fabia.

But he knew, that in fact the word that sprang to his mind almost together with "beauty" was "love"!

Chapter Five

As the Duke and Fabia rode back towards Queen's Hoo he thought he had never enjoyed an afternoon more.

They had set off after an early luncheon to visit some of the more distant parts of the Estate and to call at several of the Alms Houses, where they found that the pensioners were obviously happy and comfortable.

Then they had stopped on the top of one of the low hills, and on an open piece of ground they challenged each other over the obedience of their horses.

The Duke had to admit, although reluctantly, that Sprite had won easily. While Perseus could do the ordinary obedience-tests of coming when he was called, standing still to attention, and even doing a slow march, Sprite had a dozen other better and more complicated tricks.

"The only excuse I can plead," he said to Fabia at the end, "is that you have had more time than I have to teach him."

She had given him a mischievous little glance that told him without words that she thought it was not only time he had needed but an expertise that came from love and of course "vibrations."

"Very well," he said almost sharply. "I admit that you have 'a way,' as my Nanny used to call it, with animals, although it was something I always believed I had myself."

"Of course you had, in those days," Fabia replied, and she knew as she spoke that it would annoy him.

"If you mention my lack of vibrations again," he said angrily, "I think I shall throw you in the stream and hold your head under! I am sick and tired of hearing about them!"

"I am sorry," she said humbly.

Then she realised he was teasing.

"It is difficult to get away from a subject in which I have been so absorbed," she said, "especially as, if you want the truth, your vibrations have become very much stronger during the last two days."

"Are you flattering me?" he challenged.

"That is something I have never done. I always tell the truth," she replied seriously, and he knew it was true.

They sat talking under the shade of the trees for quite a long time while Perseus and Sprite cropped the grass.

When finally they started on the ride home, the Duke thought he had never before spent such a long time with a woman talking to her on subjects which, although unusual, he had to admit he found intriguing.

If he had been here with any of the beauties he pursued in London or elsewhere, they would have been flirting with him, keeping his attention focused on themselves, and of course wanting him to make love to them.

He was sure that because Fabia had lived such a quiet life in the country she had no idea that she might talk in a different way or behave in a different manner because she was with a man.

"She is very young and very innocent," he told himself, and wondered what she would be like when she was awakened to womanhood.

It struck him that this might cause her fairy-tale fantasy-world to disappear.

'It would be a pity,' he thought, 'because it means

so much to her, although it is of course unusual to say the least of it.'

The Duke avoided the word "supernatural," although that was what it really was, and he was certain that once Fabia lived a normal life she would approach everything in a mundane manner like other women.

They rode side by side, and without putting it into words the Duke knew that they were both appreciating the beauty of the countryside.

The sun was shining through the thick branches of the trees in the woods, making golden patterns on the mossy ground, and the banks of streams they passed were yellow with irises and kingcups.

Then at last Queen's Hoo was in sight, and once again it was looking so beautiful that the Duke felt his heart lift at the sight of it.

"I have been so happy the last two days," Fabia said, "and I think, Your Grace, you have been happy too."

"It is something about which I would not wish to argue," the Duke replied. "And I will admit that like Perseus I feel content, and glad too that tomorrow is another day."

She smiled in a way that told him she knew he was deliberately restraining himself from being more effusive.

She dismounted, patted Sprite on the neck, and ran upstairs to change from her riding-habit into a cool gown.

"What you ought to do is have a rest!" Hannah said as she helped her change.

"Rest? Why should I do that," Fabia asked, "when there are so many thrilling and exciting things to do?"

The way she spoke and the radiance in her face made Hannah draw in her breath, but she only said in a matter-of-fact voice:

"You may as well make the most of His Grace's visit. I don't suppose he'll stay long."

Fabia was still.

"Why should you say that?"

"I overheard his Valet, who knows him well, say that His Grace gets bored more quickly than any other gentleman he's ever known."

There was a little pause before Fabia said:

"I do not think His Grace is bored yet, and how could he be bored at Queen's Hoo?"

She did not wait for Hannah's reply but ran downstairs, eager to join the Duke, who she was sure would be in the Library.

As she entered he was standing in front of the bookcase which contained all the volumes which concerned the Minster family.

He held a book in his hand, and as she hurried towards him he said:

"I see that one of my relatives was such a fire-eater that he boasts of practically winning a war single-handed! I cannot believe that you wish me to follow his example!"

Fabia glanced at the book in his hand and said:

"As a Commander he was impetuous and his impetuosity cost the lives of many men."

The Duke turned over a few pages and she added:

"War is wicked, cruel, and wrong. At the same time, I can understand why men enjoy it."

"Enjoy it?" the Duke questioned.

"It is a way of proving themselves," Fabia said. "I think it is in a man's nature to struggle for achievement, and war is an easy way of doing so."

The Duke thought this over for a moment and realised that because since he had grown up there had been no wars for him to fight, he had instead striven to excel on the race-course.

As if Fabia was following his thoughts she asked:

"How often do you speak in the House of Lords?"

"I have no wish to be a politician," the Duke replied sharply.

"At the same time, it could give you a platform for

fighting for the things which are important for the
country, and people would listen to you."

The Duke looked at her with a smile.

"I thought it was this house that was supposed to
spur me on to deeds of valour, not you!"

"Perhaps I am only interpreting what the house is
saying to you," Fabia said. "If you read all these books,
the message is set down quite clearly over hundreds of
years."

The Duke looked at the packed shelves.

"It would take too long," he said at length, "and
undoubtedly I should find such reading boring after the
first two or three volumes."

"That is where you are mistaken . . ." Fabia began.

As she spoke, the door opened and Barker announced:

"Major Bicester, Your Grace, and two ladies!"

The Duke turned sharply towards the door, and as
Eddie came into the room followed by two glamorous,
decidedly over-dressed but exceedingly attractive wom-
en, he gave an exclamation.

"Eddie! I did not expect you for a least another
three days!"

"You sent me such an obvious cry for help," Eddie
replied, "that I felt I must answer it, and actually the
Boxing Championships were postponed."

He shook the Duke by the hand, then looked with
undisguised curiosity at Fabia.

Before the Duke could speak, Gigi ran eagerly to
him to slip her arm through his.

"It's very exciting to be there," she said, "and
Bettsy and I are thrilled that you've invited us! We'll
soon cheer you up and you'll no longer feel bored."

She spoke effusively with her fascinating accent,
and her dark, rather mysterious eyes looked up at him
invitingly, her red lips curved provocatively.

Bettsy took hold of his other arm.

"I've never stayed with a real live Duke before," she
said, "but I expect we can make things hum round

here, even though I find the country a bit depressing."

The Duke from long experience managed to extricate himself from their clinging hands and said to Eddie:

"I do not think, Eddie, you have met a relative of mine, Miss Fabia Wilton—Major Edward Bicester."

The Duke knew as he spoke the word "relative" that Eddie was surprised not only because Fabia was so young and beautiful but also because he had expected to find the Duke alone and was wondering how her presence would complicate matters.

It was something which was also causing the Duke some concern and he knew it was a problem that would now have to be solved.

Everything he had done since arriving at Queen's Hoo had been so interesting that he had really forgotten the letter he had sent to Eddie in desperation the evening he had stayed at the Inn near Oxford.

If it had crossed his mind, he would have supposed he had plenty of time to cancel his invitations to Gigi and Bettsy before Eddie arrived with them.

Now it was too late. They were here and already he was wondering what he should do.

Without waiting for an introduction, Gigi was already talking to Fabia.

"Do you live round here?" she asked. "Or are you also a guest?"

As she spoke she glanced at Fabia's gown, and it was obvious that she knew it was cheap and homemade and far from fashionable.

Fabia, on the other hand, was very conscious that the two ladies who had just arrived were very unlike any woman she had ever seen before in her whole life.

They wore elaborate silk travelling-cloaks in vivid colours, and their bonnets were decorated with feathers and flowers.

Both the women wore flashy jewellery which she thought looked strange in the daytime, and she had never thought any lady would use so much powder, rouge and lip-salve.

"I live here," she replied.

"All the year round?" Gigi asked. "Then I'm real sorry for you, except of course there's plenty of space for riding."

"There is certainly that," Bettsy agreed, "but there's not much of an audience, and that's something I couldn't do without!"

Bettsy laughed as she spoke and somehow it seemed a rather vulgar sound.

Fabia turned to the Duke.

"If these ladies are staying," she said, "shall I go tell Mrs. Feather to prepare bedrooms fot them?"

"Yes, of course," the Duke replied.

He realised that Fabia wished to get away and he thought it a good idea. But when Fabia turned towards the door she was already aware that Gigi had once again linked her arm through the Duke's.

"I hope I have a comfortable room," she said, "and you know where it has to be situated."

Because she was surprised at what she had heard her say, Fabia looked back.

She saw Gigi with her face turned up to the Duke's and her lips near to his.

At the moment Fabia merely thought it a very strange way of behaving.

Then as she left the Library and walked down the passage she told herself that now that the Duke had his friends to amuse him he would no longer need her.

The thought was like a stab to her heart, and as she walked up the stairs to find Mrs. Feather she knew that the happiness she had felt until a few minutes ago had vanished, and it seemed too as if the sunshine had gone behind the clouds.

She found, as she might have expected, that Mrs. Feather was in one of the bedrooms, superintending the unpacking of a trunk which had already been brought upstairs by the footmen.

The housemaid had just taken out a night-dress which strangely enough was black and was holding it up for Mrs. Feather's inspection.

Fabia stood in the door was before they realised she was there and she heard Mrs. Feather remark:

"I don't know what Her Grace'd say, that I don't!"

"If you ask me," the housemaid replied, who was down on her knees in front of the trunk, "women who ain't no better than they ought to be have no right to be staying here!"

Before Mrs. Feather could reply, Fabia, feeling that she was listening to what was not intended for her ears, walked towards them.

"I came upstairs, Mrs. Feather, to tell you that some guests have arrived," she said, "but I see you know that already."

"I do indeed, Miss!" Mrs. Feather replied.

As she spoke, Fabia saw the housemaid take some very brightly coloured underclothes from the trunk but quickly put them back again in an effort to prevent her from seeing them.

She was too late. Fabia had already noticed the cheap lace, the pink ribbons, and materials so fine that the garments were obviously transparent.

Quite suddenly she felt very young and inexperienced.

If that was what the Duke liked and those were the sort of women he admired, no wonder his Valet expected him to soon be bored by being alone with only her.

She left the bedroom and hurried down the passage, and as she did so she kept thinking of how exciting it had been to talk to the Duke, to argue with him, and to be alone with him.

Now it was all spoilt and she felt like crying.

Because it was something she had done before when she felt upset, she went along the passage to where at the very far end on the south side of the house were the rooms that had always been occupied by the Duchess.

They had been left exactly as they had been during her lifetime.

As Fabia opened the door there was the sweet fragrance of the flowers she put there every week, and also the scent of lilies, which was a perfume Her Grace had made particularly her own.

There were two rooms, a bedroom and a Sitting-Room where the Duchess always sat in the window so that she could look out onto the garden and the woods beyond.

The sun-blinds were down, but the room was still bright because the curtains were not drawn.

As Fabia walked to where the Duchess had always sat, she felt as if she were eight years old again and coming into the room for the first time with her mother soon after they had arrived at the Manor.

"This is Fabia, Your Grace!" her mother had said, and the Duchess held out her hand, saying:

"What a lovely child! She is very like you, Elizabeth."

Fabia had curtseyed. Then the Duchess had taken her small hand in hers, and she remembered how she had felt a tingling vibration which she had never forgotten.

After that the Duchess had drawn her almost like a magnet and every day she made some excuse to ride from the Manor on her pony to visit Queen's Hoo and the lady who lived there.

"Please, Mama, may I take the flowers I have picked to Her Grace?"

"Can I show Her Grace my painting I have just finished?"

"Can I tell Her Grace about the robin's-nest I found this morning?"

There was always something she wanted to show the Duchess.

Looking back now, Fabia realised that although she was only eight she had talked to her as if she were grown up, and the Duchess had seemed to enjoy her company and would reminisce about the past as if she were a contemporary.

It was a strange relationship but a very rewarding one, and Fabia thought now that the Duke had somehow stepped into the place in her life which had been empty since his grandmother had died.

She sat down in the chair next to the one the Duchess had always occupied, and she felt as if she were talking to the older woman, telling her what had happened and how suddenly she had lost the Duke when she least expected it.

It was then, as she waited, as it were, for the Duchess to answer her, that she knew she loved him.

It was such a surprising idea that for a moment Fabia thought she must be mistaken.

Then she knew that despite what she had said, despite the fact that she thought the Duke gave out no "vibrations," as she knew them, there was something about him that compelled her to be aware of him.

"It cannot be true!" she said aloud, as if the Duchess were listening. "How can I be in love with a man who is not in love with me?"

It was all so childish, but like the "Sleeping Beauty" as the Duke had called her when he first found her in the Temple, she had believed that only when a man had awakened a woman to love and had given her his heart was she ready to offer him hers in return.

Now Fabia knew almost despairingly that what she felt for the Duke he did not feel for her, and the sort of women who interested him were those downstairs, of whom she was sure neither her mother nor the Duchess would have approved.

"What can I do?" she asked.

She thought that the Duchess smiled.

"What you are saying," Fabia went on, "is that if it is ordained that we should mean anything to each other, it will happen. If not, he will go away and I shall be alone again."

She paused before she continued:

"I have been so happy here with you in the house, but now when I am alone I shall miss him, and things can never be the same again."

She gave a little sob, then without really meaning to she went down on her knees beside the chair in which the Duchess had always sat.

"Please... please... help me!"

It was a cry from her heart, and when she felt as if the Duchess laid her hand on her head, it was a comfort beyond words.

Fabia stayed for a long time in the Duchess's room, and when she left it she went to the other side of the house, where her own bedroom was situated and Hannah slept next door.

There was also a Sitting-Room attached, where Hannah sat and sewed and where Fabia, before the Duke had arrived, had often read aloud to her.

The Sitting-Room came first in the passage, and as Fabia neared the door, intent on going to her own bedroom, to her surprise she heard the Duke's voice, and she stopped still.

"I'll tell Miss Fabia what Your Grace has said," she heard Hannah say. "As it happens, I was going to suggest the same thing if Your Grace hadn't said it first."

"I am quite capable," the Duke replied in a cold tone which Fabia knew meant he was angry, "of deciding what is right or wrong for somebody who is a relation."

"Of course, Your Grace," Hannah said in a more conciliatory tone.

The way she spoke told Fabia that she was pleased at having got her own way.

"As I do not know where Miss Fabia is," the Duke said, "I will send a servant to find her and say that she is to come upstairs to you."

"Thank you, Your Grace," Hannah replied.

Fabia realised that the Duke would now leave the Sitting-Room, and as she did not wish him to think she had been eavesdropping she hurried into her own bedroom.

Just as she was closing the door she heard his footsteps going down the passage, and then she went into the Sitting-Room.

"What have you been saying?" she asked.

"His Grace came to tell you that you are to stay here with me and will have supper here tonight," Hannah replied.

"Why? Why does he not want me downstairs?" Fabia asked.

There was silence and she knew that Hanna had no wish to answer her question.

But she waited and at last, after a long pause, Hannah said:

"His Grace's—friends have come to stay."

"Yes, I know that," Fabia answered. "I have met them."

"You have met them?" Hannah asked sharply. "His Grace had no right to introduce you to such scum! What your mother would say, I don't know!"

These were almost the same words that had been used by Mrs. Feather, and Fabia asked:

"As the ladies are very smart and pretty, are they actresses?"

She knew that actresses were considered "fast" and that to go on the stage was something no Lady would do.

"I believe they ride horses as a—profession," Hannah replied almost as if the words were dragged from her lips.

"They ride horses?" Fabia cried. "Oh, I wish I had known that! Then we shall certainly have something in common."

"Over my dead body!" Hannah said sharply. "And let me make this quite clear, Miss Fabia: if you don't do what His Grace tells you, I'll take you away immediately!"

"Take me away? But where could we go?"

"That's immaterial," Hannah answered, "but I will not have you associating with women like that."

"Like what?"

This was obviously another question Hannah did not want to answer, and after a moment she said:

"You are a Lady born and bred, and those creatures should stay in the gutter where they belong!"

"But the Duke must want them here . . . perhaps to break in the new horses which are arriving from Leiscestershire? He told me he was expecting them."

Fabia felt this explanation seemed logical. At the same time, she had seen the way one of the women had looked up at him when she was in the Library, clinging close to his arm, and it seemed a strange way for an employee to behave.

"There's nothing more to be said," Hannah snapped. "You are to stay up here and, on His Grace's orders, have supper with me."

As she spoke Hannah picked up her sewing and went from the Sitting-Room through the communicating-door which led into her bedroom.

Fabia walked to the window, feeling bewildered but at the same time not so depressed as she had been at first.

If the women downstairs had come to ride the Duke's horses, she supposed they were in the same category as jockeys or grooms or any of those who looked after and raced his horses.

It was indeed strange that they should be so smartly dressed, but perhaps they were able to earn a lot of money by riding, and they would naturally want to look their best when they were coming to stay at Queen's Hoo.

At the same time, their arrival had meant that she had been turned out of the Dining-Room and would not see the Duke at all except perhaps riding with them in the distance, and that thought was unbearably depressing.

Without really meaning to, she felt herself calling

out to him, sending out wave upon wave of vibrations to remind him that she was here and, although it was hopeless, she loved him.

* * *

The meal that was brought upstairs to Fabia and Hannah was very much the same as that which had been taken into the Dining-Room, and although Hannah obviously enjoyed it, Fabia found that she was not hungry.

She kept thinking of how interesting it would be downstairs to hear them talking and laughing, and she was sure that much of the conversation would be about horses.

She also knew she would have liked to watch the Duke sitting at the top of the table as she had seen him these past evenings, looking magnificent and very much at his ease in the big carved chair that she felt looked like a throne.

When the Duchess had talked of the Kings and Queens who had been her guests, Fabia had always imagined them sitting in that particular chair, which had been acquired in the reign of Charles II and was surmounted by a crown supported by cupids and beneath it a heart.

Never had she imagined that any man could be so handsome or so authoritative as the Duke, and yet until now she had never thought of him as somebody she could love. She could only admire him as she had admired his grandmother and his other relatives about whom she had read in the books in the Library.

'I felt sure,' she thought to herself, 'that I would never love anybody unless their vibrations linked with mine and we were joined by something mystical and wonderful which is part of life itself.'

When supper was finished Hannah left the Sitting-Room to fetch her sewing, which she had left behind in her bedroom, and that gave Fabia the opportunity she was waiting for to escape.

She knew there was only one place she could go, one place where she could think and try to understand the new sensations which were pulsating through her body and which were so different from anything she had ever known before.

She slipped down a side staircase and out through a door leading to the garden, then ran across the lawn, past the Water Garden, and into the shadows of the shrubs.

She was breathless by the time she reached the Temple, and she sat down on the steps to lean her head against the pillar as she had done so often before and look out at the vista in front of her.

The sun was sinking in a last blaze of glory behind the trees in the Park. The stars were already twinkling overhead and everything seemed to have a magical golden glow about it, except where the shadows were deep purple under the trees.

"It is so lovely!" Fabia told herself. "And since it belongs to the Duke and is part of him, how can I help loving him?"

She had answered her own question.

She had actually, she knew now, loved him ever since she had been aware of him as a small boy laughing here in the Temple and running through the woods.

Looking back, it was hard to remember when she had first known he was there.

It must have been soon after they came to live in the Manor and she was constantly at Queen's Hoo.

Sometimes she thought she saw him, at other times it seemed as if he were beside her, laughing, shouting with joy, dodging through the trees, or racing across the lawn.

'It was so vivid because he was so alive,' she thought.

Even though she loved the Duke she could not pretend that he had now the same sparkling personality that had been his when he was young.

"Queen's Hoo will bring it back to him," she reassured herself.

She thought that all those who had lived here and from here had projected their influence out into the world had become leaders and heroes, men of success and achievement in one direction or another.

'That is what he must do,' she thought.

Howver much the servants praised him, her instinct told her there was something lacking, although it was hard to define exactly what it was.

She was thinking of him so insistently that it was no surprise when suddenly, when it was almost dark except for the stars and the rising moon, he appeared along the path between the shrubs and came to the Temple.

"I knew I would find you here," he said.

Fabia did not answer.

She was merely aware that her heart had leapt in her breast and she felt as if a streak of moonlight ran through her whole body, making it glow with an iridescent light that she could see and feel.

The Duke lowered himself to sit down on the step beside her.

He looked at the house below them, the lights blazing golden in the windows and the last glimmer of sunlight disappearing behind the trees.

"I am sorry, Fabia."

"About what?"

"I had forgotten that I had invited my friend Eddie Bicester here to stay and had told him to bring two—ladies with him."

There was a short pause before the word "ladies," and Fabia said:

"I hear they are riders. Are they very good on horses?"

There was a wistful note in her voice which told the Duke that she was thinking they perhaps rode better than she did, and he smiled before he replied:

"Yes, they are very good, but I do not think you need fear any rivals in that field."

"I am . . . glad."

"They will be leaving tomorrow because they have an engagement in London which they have to fulfil."

This was untrue, but the Duke thought it was the best explanation he could give, and in fact he had already told Eddie that they were to leave and he would recompense them generously for the trouble they had gone to in coming here.

"Good Heavens!" Eddie had exclaimed. "I cannot send them away for at least four or five days, and incidentally it has cost them quite a lot of money to come here. The owner of the Livery Stable was very reluctant to let them go."

"That is immaterial," the Duke had said, "and I want no arguments about it, Eddie. You brought them, and you can tell them that our arrangements have been changed, and a nice fat cheque will doubtless soften the blow."

"Well, really, Vian! I call this extremely high-handed and positively insulting!"

Eddie stopped speaking for a moment, then said:

"Has this anything to do with your very pretty relation who I had no idea was staying here with you?"

"She is living at Queen's Hoo with her old maid-servant, and it is certainly embarrassing that I cannot allow her to mix with Gigi and Bettsy," the Duke replied evasively.

He was aware that Eddie was looking at him searchingly, and he said quickly:

"As you are so interested, it is nothing like that. Fabia is a nice child, and I found her staying here when I arrived. As she is a distant cousin, I naturally feel responsible for whom she meets, and 'Pretty Horse-Breakers' are not the right company for a débutante."

"No, of course not," Eddie agreed, "but it seems strange that she should have been living here without your being aware of it."

"I thought that myself," the Duke answered, "but there is no time to talk about it now. Just get rid of Gigi and Bettsy without any fuss."

"I thought Gigi interested you," Eddie said. "She is certainly very attractive and I imagine much easier to handle than Dilys. She certainly will not try to marry you!"

This was what the Duke had thought himself, but as he remembered it, it seemed a very long time ago.

"I will make it up to Gigi when I return to London," the Duke said. "The question is, when will that be?"

"As there is no answer to that, I imagined that was why you asked me to bring her here to you."

"I do not intend to discuss it," the Duke said loftily. "Do as I ask, Eddie, and send them back."

Eddie sighed.

"I must say you strain our friendship sometimes to breaking-point, Vian," he said. "Another time I will insist on your doing your own dirty work!"

The Duke had not replied.

He had merely left Eddie's bedroom, where they had been talking, and gone downstairs to the Drawing-Room, where they were meeting before dinner and where the two women were waiting for them.

As he looked at them he realised how deplorably in their evening-gowns with outrageously low décolletages they jarred with the pictures on the wall, the flowers on the table arranged by Fabia, and the beauty of the garden outside where dusk was just falling.

It was over dinner that he became more and more aware of the mistake he had made in bringing them to Queen's Hoo. Their presence was something so utterly alien that, for perhaps the first time in his life, the Duke felt ashamed because he had shown a lack of good taste.

As Gigi flattered him, fluttering her long masca-raed eye-lashes, pouting her lips provocatively, and making every excuse to touch him, he was acutely aware that Fabia had sat previously in the same chair.

Then they had talked of things which had interested him, and he could almost feel she was there beside him.

"It is those damned vibrations again!" he thought to himself.

But he knew that she had been correct in saying that he could feel them, and at dinner they seemed to be preventing him from hearing what Gigi was saying, not that it was worth listening to.

At the same time, the Duke felt more and more disgusted by the manner in which she tried to attract him.

"I am being ridiculous!" he tried to tell himself.

But he knew he was fighting a losing battle in trying to behave as he would have done before he came to Queen's Hoo.

There was no doubt that Eddie was well amused and certainly attracted by Bettsy.

By the time the meal was over they were talking in low, intimate voices, toasting each other, and from the expression in their eyes it was quite obvious what would happen later in the evening.

He had of course expected the same for himself, but as soon as the women left the Dining-Room and the Duke and Eddie were alone with their port, the Duke said:

"Amuse the women, Eddie, until I come back."

"Where are you going?" Eddie asked sharply.

The Duke had already reached the door, and either he did not hear the question or he had no intention of answering it.

He did not have to think where Fabia was likely to be; he knew.

As he walked across the lawn he felt the irritation that had been rising within him during dinner subside, and it was as if he stepped back into the peace and magic of Queen's Hoo and left behind the other world which had temporarily encroached on him.

He did not hurry, because he knew he had plenty of time.

He stopped for a moment at the Water Garden to listen to the soft music of the cascade falling onto the goldfish-bowl before he walked on.

As he reached the Temple he saw it was suffused with light, and there was a reflection of the stars in Fabia's eyes as she looked up at him and he sat down beside her.

"This is what I have been wanting to do," he told himself, "ever since I came home."

Because he did not wish to interpret the last word literally, he quickly explained to himself that it was the Temple which had attracted him as it always had.

Fabia's interest in it was coincidental except that there was a rightness about her being there because it was where he had found her on the first day of his arrival.

They talked for a few minutes, then sat in silence, both staring out over the garden, both somehow content to be side by side so that there was no need for words.

The Duke felt as if this was all he ever asked of her, the quietness, the peace, the knowledge that nothing else was of any importance.

He could forget here the Queen's displeasure, the disapproval of his relatives, and the problem of Gigi waiting for him to come back to the house and behave in a manner which he had no intention of doing.

He gave a little sigh of contentment and without really meaning to said aloud:

"This is all I ever want, and as I have it, why should I worry about anything else?"

There was a pause before Fabia answered:

"Because it is . . . not enough for you . . . and never will be."

It was as though she had thrown a glass of water over him, and the Duke stiffened as he asked:

"Why should you say that?"

"Because you are too intelligent not to be aware that at this moment you are lulling yourself into a feeling of safety and security."

"But that is what I want!"

Although it was dark, he knew she shook her head.

"How can you know so much about me?"

"Because before you came I was thinking of you as you were, and that is the real you: the boy I knew, who would always have been ready to act heroically."

"I still feel like that at times," the Duke said.

Fabia did not answer, but he knew she was not impressed.

"Then what do you suggest I do?" he asked crossly.

There was silence for a moment. Then Fabia said:

"If you stay here, then I am sure, in fact I am certain, that an opportunity will come to you to do something great, something that is important not only to you but to other people."

"Are you fortune-telling?"

"I am looking into your future."

"This is a talent I had not suspected," he said sarcastically.

"It is not something I can do very often, but now, perhaps because we are sitting in the Temple, I can see that you will rule over many people and it will be a position in which you will have great authority and the power to do good."

The Duke tried to laugh lightly.

"Are you imagining that somebody might offer me one of those shaky European Kingdoms whose thrones are always empty and looking for an occupant?"

As he spoke he was thinking of Greece and Belgium, the thrones of which had been hawked round the younger Princes of Royal Houses.

"I do not think it is that," Fabia said, "but I know it will happen, and I think that when it does you will do what is right and what your grandmother would wish you to do."

As she spoke she felt as if the Duchess had put the words into her mouth rather than that they were her own, and she added pleadingly:

"Please ... please ... when the offer comes to you, remember it is a position in which you will be able to carry on the traditions of the family."

The Duke turned his head to look at her, meaning to answer sharply that he did not believe a word of her prognostications and anyway it was very unlikely that he would occupy any greater position than the one he held at the moment.

Then as he looked at Fabia in the light from the Heavens, he thought that she looked not only very lovely but insubstantial, unreal, and she might in fact be a spirit of the Temple itself.

"You frighten me," he said in a low voice. "If I were wise I would leave Queen's Hoo immediately and never come back."

"Why should you want to do that?"

"Because you are disrupting my life. You are trying to change it, and I am not certain that is something I want or will enjoy."

Fabia looked at him for a long moment. Then she held out her hand.

"Let me feel the change."

Just for a moment the Duke hesitated as if he was afraid. Then he put his hand in hers.

Her fingers were cool, and once again when he touched them he felt the strange vibrations he had felt before.

Then her palm was close against his, and he felt for the first time so physically aware of her that he thought she must feel the same about him.

But she was silent, and after a moment he asked:

"Well? What is the verdict?"

"They are there," she said, "when they were not there before. But you are fighting against them and they are finding it difficult, very difficult, to prevail against such restraint."

The Duke disengaged his hand from Fabia's.

"That is not very encouraging."

"I want it to be," she said in a low voice. "I want to encourage you as your grandmother would have done."

The Duke rose to his feet.

"My grandmother is not here," he said, "and you

depress me with your talk of the future. I think I would be wise to enjoy myself for the present. After all, that is tangible and real, and certainly it is more encouraging."

As he spoke he walked away and disappeared into the darkness of the shrubs.

Fabia watched him go. Then she gave a little sigh that seemed to come from the very depths of her being as she put her hands up to her eyes.

She was not crying.

She was only thinking despairingly that she had failed the Duke and his grandmother and her own love for him.

Chapter Six

The Duke walked back to the house.

Because he was feeling annoyed and disturbed, he went in by the garden-door, and instead of going into the Drawing-Room, where he was certain Eddie was with the two women, he went to the Library.

Even there he felt conscious of the bookcases filled with the history of the family, and he thought absurdly that they were attracting his attention, or rather, in Fabia's words, vibrating towards him.

He flung himself down in an armchair and tried to sort out his feelings.

He told himself that the house was depressing and that living in the country without his usual amusements was getting him down and the sooner he went to Paris or somewhere similar the better.

At the same time, he could hear Fabia's soft voice telling him that a chance would come to him to do something great, and he told himself cynically that at least it would be a change.

He was not an introspective person as a rule, and yet now that he looked back on his life, although he had thought it was full and complete, he was too intelligent not to know that it was nothing of the kind.

What did he really want?

The answer which came into his mind was: "A goal," and he knew that if he was to attain anything worthwhile it must be something to benefit not only himself personally but other people as well.

That was what Fabia was wishing for him!

But then he asked himself angrily how he could listen to a young girl who lived alone in the country and expect her to understand the complexity of his existence.

At the same time, he knew she had awakened his critical faculty and now he was analysing everything he did and, what was most unusual, himself.

"Dammit all, I shall leave for Paris tomorrow," he decided, "or the South of France or anywhere else, as long as I am away from this house!"

He sat for a long time deliberately planning where he would go, what he would do, and whom he would take with him.

For some reason he could not understand, Gigi was not included in his plans, nor were any of the beauties he had known in London. Not that most of them would have been able to go anywhere with him, except of course for Dilys.

"What I need is pastures new," he said aloud.

There was a note of bravado in his voice, as if he defied the fates to unite against him.

As he spoke the door opened and Eddie came into the Library.

He looked round, saw that the Duke was alone, and said:

"Talking to yourself, Vian? I suppose you know it is a sign of insanity?"

"I shall go insane if I have to stay here much longer," the Duke answered. "What has happened?"

Eddie sat down in a chair opposite his friend.

"Actually it is not as bad as I had anticipated."

"Why not?"

There was a pause before Eddie replied:

"Gigi is quite convinced you will change your mind before . . . tomorrow morning."

The Duke grasped the implication of what Eddie was saying and merely remarked:

"She will be disappointed. I intend them to leave. I suppose you assured them both that I will be generous in recompense for any inconvenience I have caused?"

"'Very generous!' were my actual words," Eddie replied.

"Good!" the Duke said. "I am going abroad. Will you come with me?"

"I would like to," Eddie answered. "But first I shall have to get permission from the Colonel. And there is something else."

"What is that?" the Duke enquired.

"I promised the women I would escort them back to London."

The Duke stared at him and then smiled.

"I imagine that was as much on your account as on mine."

Eddie looked slightly embarrassed.

"As it happens, I feel rather committed where Bettsy is concerned."

"I thought you would be," the Duke said. "Well, I will wait for you, but not more than two or three days. I could not stand this place any longer than that!"

Eddie was about to ask him what was wrong, then changed his mind.

"Where are you thinking of going?" he asked after an uncomfortable silence.

"Anywhere that is amusing," the Duke replied. "Paris or perhaps the South of France."

"It will be too hot," Eddie stated. "What about staying with some of your friends who live in those large, comfortable *Châteaux?* I remember when you have entertained them in London and Minster they have always been most persistent in inviting you back."

"It is certainly an idea," the Duke agreed.

He rose to his feet to walk restlessly about the room. Then he said:

"I should have a good mind to go back to London and to hell with the Queen! Why should she order me about? I certainly have no wish to take up my duties at the Palace, but I am more comfortable in my own London house than anywhere else."

"You know as well as I do that you cannot go against a Royal Command," Eddie said. "You are in disgrace, Vian, and for the next two months London is out-of-bounds."

"Then I shall go to Minster."

"I am sure Dilys will be delighted to join you there!"

There was silence and the Duke suddenly kicked across the room a stool that was in his path.

"I am fed up and bored!" he said. "For God's sake, Eddie, let us leave tomorrow. Bettsy will not run away. She will be waiting when you return."

There was silence again, before Eddie replied:

"I do not know what has upset you, Vian, but for the first time since I have known you—and that is a long time—you are behaving like a spoilt child! I am only glad nobody else can see you."

The Duke stared at him incredulously as if he could not believe his ears, and Eddie went on:

"I admire you so much, just as everybody else does. But, as you must be aware, you cannot do anything which could have repercussions not only on yourself but on your family."

The Duke made an incoherent sound but did not interrupt, and Eddie continued:

"You have got yourself into a mess, so you must take the consequences like the sportsman you have always been. But that certainly does not necessitate making things worse than they are already."

"All right! All right!" the Duke said irritably. "I see your point, but I still intend to leave here."

"There is nothing to stop you," Eddie replied, "but I tell you quite frankly you are more comfortable here than you are likely to be anywhere else at this time of the year. If you want to sizzle like a sausage we will go to the South of France, or wherever else takes your fancy, but do not expect me to like it!"

"Very well," the Duke said. "I will take you somewhere where you will not sizzle. But if you must play the galant to Bettsy, hurry back to me as quickly as you can."

"I promise," Eddie replied. "And it is lucky that I am in the Colonel's good books at the moment."

He glanced at the clock on the mantelpiece and said:

"I am going to bed. I am tired after driving your horses, excellent though they are, and I am not particularly looking forward to doing the same journey again tomorrow."

He rose to his feet and the Duke said:

"I am grateful to you, Eddie, and in the future I will not forget to make up for what you have done."

Eddie looked at the Duke for a moment, then he said:

"There is one other thing I want to know. What are you going to do about that alluring relative of yours? And by the way, if she is staying here alone, should she not have a Chaperone?"

"That is something I am going to arrange before I leave," the Duke said.

"I have never seen such a haunting face!" Eddie said as if he was talking to himself.

"Haunting?"

"Well, perhaps that is the wrong word. Alluring, if you like—no, that is not right either—but she is different from any woman I have ever seen, and very lovely."

"And also very young," the Duke observed in an uncompromising tone.

"She will grow up," Eddie remarked, "and whatever her age, there will be no difficulty in finding her a husband."

"That is a problem which does not concern me."

"No, of course not. At the same time, I cannot

help feeling that the reason you are determined to get rid of Gigi and Bettsy is that she is here."

The Duke thought that was the obvious deduction Eddie would make. But because he could not think of a plausible answer that would not suggest that he was perjuring himself, he merely remarked:

"I will do what is right for Fabia, and everything will be arranged before we leave here."

"I shall look forward to meeting her again," Eddie said. "What explanation did you make to her for not inviting her to join us for dinner?"

Because he was being asked unwelcome questions, the Duke's temper flared again.

"For Heaven's sake, Eddie!" he said. "Do I have to give you account for everything I do?"

Eddie looked across the room at his friend and raised his eye-brows.

"Good-night, Vian," he said. "I hope you *sleep* well."

He accentuated the word "sleep," and as he went from the Library he thought the Duke would follow him.

But when left alone the Duke wandered round the room for a time before he decided that he might as well go to bed.

As he reached the Hall the footmen were extinguishing some of the lights and a nightwatchman was already on duty.

He went up the stairs and along the passage which led to his bedroom.

He had no idea in which room Gigi was sleeping, and he told himself he had no need to know and if she was waiting for him she would wait in vain.

He knew exactly what she had meant when she had said to Eddie that he would change his mind before tomorrow morning.

He reached the door of his own room, but as he put out his hand to open it a feeling he could not explain came over him so strongly that it brought him to a standstill. It was almost as if somebody was beside him, warning him that it would be a mistake to go into his bedroom.

"If Gigi is there," he told himself, "which is unlikely, I shall merely turn her out."

But as he thought of it he knew that would be difficult.

Anybody as experienced as Gigi would be bound to ensure that he desired her physically, whatever he felt about her in any other aspect.

"Do not go into your room!"

He could almost hear a voice warning him aloud.

Then, inexplicably, as if she were actually there, he found himself thinking of his grandmother.

He had the unaccountable conviction that she was beside him, saving him, forestalling something which would appeal to all that was lowest in his nature, when in her lifetime she had stood for everything that was highest.

"It is the atmosphere of this house," the Duke told himself as if dismissing the idea.

Once again he put out his hand towards the door, even though as he did so he knew it was just a gesture and he would not open it.

Then, as if the memory of his grandmother compelled him to do so, he walked away and almost unconsciously went towards the South Wing, where her rooms were situated.

He opened the outer door and went into the small Hall where there were two doors, one which led into the Sitting-Room and one to her bedroom.

It was dark but he did not hesitate, and opening her bedroom door he went into the room he had not entered for ten years.

He was instantly conscious of the fragrance of the flowers and the sweet scent of lilies that he had always associated with his grandmother.

The room was not completely in darkness.

The moonlight was silver on either side of the long

curtains which covered the windows and there was enough light to guide him across the room.

He pulled back two of the curtains and opened a diamond-paned casement.

Then as the soft warmth of the night air was on his face and the moonlight almost blinded his eyes with its radiance, he turned round to look at the room behind him.

There was the huge bed with its curtains of blue silk and its dome of carved gold surmounted by doves.

It was not an Elizabethan bed like that in which Queen Elizabeth had slept. It was a French bed that had come to the house during the reign of Charles II.

It had always seemed a perfect background for his grandmother, and the Duke felt now as if she were in the room, waiting for him to talk to her.

He found himself instinctively listening for her voice and her laughter, which had been a sound of sheer music.

Suddenly, feeling she had drawn him here to take him away from whatever danger was waiting for him in his own bedroom, he knew where he would stay the night.

He took off his coat and undid his cravat, then the first few buttons on his shirt.

Because he had been dining not with Ladies but with women like Gigi and Bettsy, he had worn a velvet smoking-jacket frogged with braid.

His shirt beneath it was made of fine linen, not starched and very much more comfortable than what he wore on more formal occasions.

He flung everything he had taken off down onto a chair by the bed, kicked off his black velvet slippers, and lay down on top of the satin cover with his head against the soft pillows.

As he did so, he felt as if he were a small boy who was obeying his grandmother's commands and as he did so was anxious to please her.

He still felt as if she were very near to him, and

because he was tired and the moonlight was bright he shut his eyes.

* * *

A long time after the Duke had left her, Fabia walked slowly back to the house.

She was aware that in upsetting the Duke she had hurt herself, and the pain of it seemed like a great stone in her breast, weighing her down with a dull heaviness which seemed to increase with every step she took.

As the Duke had done, she let herself in through the garden-door and walked up the secondary staircase, which led to the floor on which her bedroom was situated.

As she walked down the passage she wondered if Hannah was worried because she had been away so long, and hoped she had been sensible enough to go to bed and not wait for her return.

She opened her bedroom door quietly and saw with relief that the room was empty and there was only one candle left alight beside the bed.

Then she heard voices from the other side of the door leading into the Sitting-Room.

The door was not quite closed and she could hear what was being said.

"Major Bicester's leaving at ten o'clock tomorrow morning to take those women back to London."

It was Mrs. Feather who spoke, and Hannah replied:

"That at least is good news."

"I agree with you," Mrs. Feather said, "but tomorrow'll be too late."

"What do you mean by that?" Hannah enquired.

Mrs. Feather's voice dropped lower so that it was almost impossible for Fabia to hear what she said.

"When I goes along to the dark one before dinner to see if she has everything she wants, I hears her asking Emily which was His Grace's bedroom."

"Did Emily tell her?" Hannah asked.

"I were too late to stop her," Mrs. Feather answered, "and it's easy to understand what she's after!"

Hannah sighed.

"I should never have brought Miss Fabia here when Mr. Durwood suggested it. But how was I to guess His Grace'd come back after being away all those years?"

"That's true enough," Mrs. Feather agreed, "and none of us could have imagined that he would bring women of that sort into the house that's sacred to his grandmother's memory."

"No, indeed!" Hannah murmured.

"I can remember His Grace when he was much younger," Mrs. Feather went on, "and a fine, upstanding young man he was. It'd break his grandmother's heart, that it would, to know what was happening to him now."

There was a sob in Mrs. Feather's voice, and as if she could not bear to hear any more Fabia very, very softly pulled the communicating-door closed without making a sound.

She undressed quickly and got into bed, blowing out the candle as she did so.

Then she turned her face against the pillow, feeling as if the pain in her heart was too much to bear.

*   *   *

The Duke was aware of a slight sound.

He had been asleep and did not open his eyes, but he tried to remember where he was.

It was the scent of flowers which made him remember what had happened and why he was sleeping not in his own bed but in his grandmother's.

Then as his mind cleared he recognised the slim slight body with the small fair head.

He wondered why Fabia should be in his grandmother's bedroom, and why tonight of all nights, when he was there.

He lay very still, knowing that she was unlikely to

see him in the shadows of the bed, and he thought anyway that in a little while she would go away without being aware of his presence.

She moved back from the window and turned sideways so that he saw her exquisite profile.

He was aware that she was looking at the chair in which his grandmother habitually sat at the window and was identical to the one she used in her Sitting-Room.

Then very softly, in a voice that sounded as if it were part of the moonlight and not real or human, he heard Fabia say:

"Help me . . . you *must* help me . . . how can . . . he spoil himself with . . . a woman like . . . that?"

There was a little pause, then she went on:

"It is wrong for him . . . because he is so fine and noble . . . and could do such . . . great things . . . if only he understood what is . . . expected of him."

There was a little pause as if she was waiting for an answer before she continued:

"You love him . . . and I know . . . I love him in the same way as you do . . . I want him to reach the heights which are only . . . possible for a man who does not waste his life and who listens to . . . the voice of . . . God."

As she finished speaking Fabia went down on her knees.

Now her hands were clasped together, her head was bent, and the Duke was aware that she was praying.

He was still watching her when suddenly it seemed to him that she was enveloped with light which came not from the moon but from Fabia herself. Simultaneously he understood everything he had tried deliberately to reject.

The knowledge seemed to sweep over him and as it did so he knew he not only understood but loved Fabia.

It was a love he had never known before, quite different from any emotion he had ever been capable of feeling. As it swept through his body not gently and quietly but with the violence of a typhoon, he felt as if it forced aside everything that had restricted and confined him in the past.

Now there was only a vivid, pulsating aliveness that he had never felt before.

Fabia raised her head and looked again at the chair as if she were seeing the Duchess sitting there.

It was then as she rose to her feet that the Duke rose too from the bed and walked towards her.

She was conscious of him before she looked in the direction from which he came, and she was very still before she turned and they looked at each other.

Her head and her whole body were haloed with light, and as she had risen the soft woollen shawl she had worn over her nightgown had dropped from her shoulders onto the floor without her noticing it.

She stood looking insubstantial, ethereal, not like a ghost but like a nymph from a stream, or perhaps a goddess come down from Olympus.

She was not human but divine, and for the moment as the Duke stood beside her he just wanted to look at her and know without words, without touching her, that they were indivisibly one.

Then in the moonlight he saw that her eyes were a little afraid in case he was still angry, and he smiled as he said very quietly:

"I think Grandmama called you here, just as she called me."

"I . . I had to . . . come."

"Because you were worried about me?"

"I . . . I was . . . afraid."

"There is no need to be," he said. "Grandmama looked after me as you asked her to do."

He knew as he spoke that Fabia remembered what she had just been saying and how revealing it had been. As her eye-lashes fluttered he was sure that the colour rose in her cheeks.

Very gently the Duke put his arms round her.

"Your pleading and your prayers have been answered."

She looked up at him.

"You mean...?"

"I mean," he said gently, "the only woman I want in my life is you, and I know now I cannot live without you. I will be everything you want me to be, if you will look after me and help me."

Fabia gave a little cry and he felt her tremble.

"I am... dreaming!" she whispered. "I know I am... dreaming!"

"And I am dreaming too," the Duke replied.

Then his lips were on hers.

At first he kissed her gently, tenderly, and for the moment without passion, because everything that had happened made him feel as if they were neither of them human but part of something sacred and divine.

Then as he felt the softness of her mouth beneath his and she moved instinctively closer to him, his arms tightened and his lips became more demanding and more insistent.

At the same time, because it was different from any kiss he had ever given before, and because he knew that for Fabia it was the first time she had been kissed, he kept himself strictly under control.

But he could not control the rapture that he had never known before with any other woman, nor the sensations that were different in a way that he could not explain to himself, except that they were an ecstasy that had nothing in common with the passion that other women had aroused in him.

It was utterly perfect, and when at last the Duke raised his head and looked down into Fabia's face, he felt as if they were both in another world which he had never known existed.

"I love you!" he said in his deep voice.

"I... love... you, too," Fabia said. "I... only realised it... today. Then when I knew I... loved you, I knew it was you who was always... with me in the... Temple. I... heard you... felt you... and that was why I was... never alone."

"That is something you will never be in the future," the Duke said. "We will be together, my darling, and I will try to be everything you want of me."

He drew in his breath and went on:

"This is living, this is life, and now I know I am really a part of the vibrations which you tell me encircle the world, and I will never, I promise you, lose them again."

Fabia gave a little cry of happiness.

She laid her head against his shoulder and said:

"Your grandmother would be . . . thrilled to hear you say that . . . in fact I am sure that she does know!"

"That is what I am thinking too," the Duke agreed, "and this was the right place for us to find each other, here in her room."

He kissed her cheek befoe he said:

"The only question is now: how soon will you marry me so we can be together and you can teach me about Heavenly love while I teach you about my love?"

"It will be the . . . real love . . . which I knew first in the Temple."

"Of course," the Duke said. "and it was in the Temple that I first found you and thought you were 'Sleeping Beauty.'"

He held her close to him as he went on:

"I did not kiss you then, but now I shall kiss you awake until I can be sure that your vibrations will never take you away from me, and that you are mine completely not only in your heart but in your mind."

"I love you with my heart and mind . . . already," Fabia whispered, "and also with my . . . spirit or soul. Everything about me is . . . yours."

"I will make sure of that," the Duke answered.

Then he was kissing her again passionately, until Fabia moved against him and said shyly:

"I . . . I have only just . . . realised that I am . . . not wearing my . . . shawl!"

As she spoke her breath was coming fitfully from between her lips, and the Duke realised that because his kisses had been fiercer and more demanding, she was becoming aware of herself as a woman and therefore shy.

As if he understood that she was very young and innocent and he must be very gentle in the way he taught her about love, he picked up her shawl from the floor and wrapped it round her.

"When I first saw you standing in the moonlight," he said, "I thought you were a nymph, then perhaps a goddess from Olympus."

"I would like to be . . . both for . . . you," Fabia replied, "but do you not think when you . . . see me again in the . . . daytime you will be . . . disappointed?"

"I am not going to answer that question," the Duke replied, "because you can answer it for yourself. Your vibrations, my precious little love, tell you far more eloquently than I can what I am feeling for you."

"I . . . I thought you never wanted to . . . hear of my . . . vibrations again!" Fabia teased.

"I have a feeling they are going to mean a great deal more to me in the future, so I will have to get used to them," the Duke said. "But if you talk about them too much I will just kiss you into silence—and that is a promise!"

"I would . . . like that," she replied. "I did not think a kiss could be so wonderful . . . so absolutely perfect . . . and yet I suppose I always knew it would be . . . if I kissed a person whose . . . vibrations linked with mine."

She glanced at him from under her eye-lashes as she spoke, and the Duke laughed.

"As long as you allow me to kiss you," he said, "I do not mind if the reason for its being so perfect as you say, and wonderful is our vibrations!"

He put his arms round her and as she lifted her lips ready for his he said:

"What is this magic about you that makes you different from every other woman I have ever known? You are very beautiful, but it is not your beauty which makes you irresistible. Therefore it must be magic, not the magic of the house, my precious, but the magic of you."

"I think the house has captured us both," Fabia said, "and I do not think we shall ever . . . escape from it."

The Duke smiled.

"I tried to do so tonight," he said, "in fact I told Eddie I intended to go abroad. I was running away, but Queen's Hoo was too strong for me, or rather you were!"

There was silence. Then Fabia said:

"If you are . . . afraid that either Queen's Hoo or I are trying to hold you . . . captive, perhaps it would be . . . wisest if you did go abroad and . . . away from us to be quite certain that we are what you want, before you . . . commit yourself any . . . further."

The Duke laughed, and it was a very tender sound.

"I know exactly what I want," he said, "I want you! I want you with me, beside me, close to me, in my arms for the rest of my life. Is that the answer?"

Fabia gave a deep sigh.

"It is the answer I want to hear, but because I love . . . you so absolutely . . . so completely . . . I want you to be . . . sure."

"I am sure," the Duke said firmly. "I have been indecisive in the past, but already you have made me a more decisive, more determined man, and I intend to have my own way, and that is all that matters."

"You are wonderful!" Fabia said. "And because I love you I will do . . . anything you ask of me . . . anything! And I will pray I will never . . . disappoint you."

The way she spoke was very moving and the Duke drew her close to him, but he did not kiss her.

Instead, his lips were against her forehead as he said:

"You are lovely! So unbelievably, incredibly lovely, my darling! I swear before God, and here in Grandmama's room, that in the future I will never fail either of you."

*   *   *

They sat talking, close in each other's arms, until the stars began to fade and the first fingers of the dawn appeared in the sky.

"I must send you to bed, my precious," the Duke said.

"And you must go to sleep too."

"I am not tired," he answered. "I feel as if I have suddenly come alive and begun to live. I never before felt so young or so full of joy!"

"At the same time, you must sleep," Fabia said, "and when your guests have gone we will make plans."

"I intend to marry you at once," the Duke said, "But not with a grand wedding with all my relations present."

Fabia did not speak. She only looked at him and he said:

"The Church here on the grounds is where I went every Sunday with my grandmother when I was a little boy. It is very old. In fact, it was built before the house was, and many of my ancestors are buried there."

"Yes, I know," Fabia said. "I have been there every Sunday since I have lived at Queen's Hoo."

"I am reviving my own memories of it," the Duke explained, "and I know, although I had never thought of it until now, that I would rather be married from that Church than anywhere else."

As he spoke, he thought of the grand Society Wedding that his friends and relations would expect him to have, but he knew that was something he would have disliked in any circumstances, and most especially when he was marrying Fabia.

They needed nothing more than the vibrations of love between themselves and the blessing of God.

It would be more real to them if they were alone instead of with a congregation where their vows would be muted and distorted by people who did not understand.

"We will be married here in the Church," the Duke said firmly. "We will begin our honeymoon at

Queen's Hoo, and then I will take you, my precious, anywhere you wish to go."

"I will go . . . anywhere as long as I am with . . . you," Fabia answered. "That is all that matters . . . that we should be . . . together."

"We will be together for always," the Duke assured her, "and, my darling, I can imagine nothing more perfect than that you should be my wife, to help and inspire me to do all those noble deeds—although I cannot think that they might be—to be recounted and included on bookshelves amongst my ancestors."

Fabia did not laugh, she merely said:

"I am convinced that one day that is what will happen."

"Are you once again telling my fortune?"

"I am stating a fact," she replied, "because I know it to be true!"

"I can see that amongst other things I shall become conceited once I am married to you."

"And there will be plenty for you to be conceited about," Fabia promised.

The Duke drew her to her feet.

"As you expect me to be authoritative and autocratic," he said, "I am now going to order you to bed, and to dream of me!"

"I could dream of nothing else tonight."

"I would be very angry and very jealous any night if I were not in your dreams."

She laughed.

"I think I am the one more likely to be jealous in the future, although even if you are surrounded and pursued by lovely ladies, I have a feeling you will always come back to me because we are not two people but one."

"That is indisputably true," the Duke said, "and, my precious, when you are there, I know I shall not be able to see any other woman's face or even realise she exists."

He spoke with a sincerity that made Fabia look up at him adoringly with a light in her eyes which he thought was so beautiful that once again he could only kiss her.

Then he drew her towards the door, and when they reached it Fabia said:

"Where will you sleep?"

"Here! We have been so ecstatically happy here tonight, my lovely wife-to-be, that I feel I want to stay with Grandmama."

The Duke spoke quite simply, and Fabia, knowing that this was something he would never have said before, was aware how deeply his love for her had changed him.

"Good-night," she whispered, "and . . . God bless you!"

The Duke kissed her again.

He opened the door of the bedroom, then the outer door.

The candles had almost gutted away in the sconces, but there was just enough light left for him to watch Fabia moving away down the long corridor.

Only when she had vanished into the shadows at the end of it and he could see her no more did the Duke go back into the bedroom and shut the door behind him.

Then he drew back the covers from the bed, pulled off his remaining clothes, and got between the sheets.

By now the sky was translucent, the stars had almost vanished, and the moon was a pale shadow of itself.

But the Duke thought that was where he and Fabia had been tonight, and it would be the first of many journeys.

"Nobody has ever been as lucky as I have been," he told himself.

He felt as if the two women who really loved him, his grandmother and Fabia, were with him as he fell asleep.

*   *   *

In her own bedroom Fabia knelt down beside the bed and said a prayer of gratitude.

"Thank You, God, Thank You!" she said. "How could I have known... how could I have guessed I would find a love so perfect and part of You?"

Then as she got into bed she felt as if the Duke's arms were round her and his lips were on hers.

With her too was the memory of the feelings he had aroused in her and the sensations she had never known existed until tonight.

She knew that it was not only love that she must give him in return, but inspiration.

For a moment she was afraid because she was so young and inexperienced in the world where he lived and where she must follow him.

Then she knew that she was not alone, and that just as his grandmother had guided and drawn the Duke to her room tonight and saved him from the temptation that was awaiting him, so would she help her.

There was also Queen's Hoo and all those who had shared her Minster blood, who had left their imprint and their vibrations behind for any member of the family to trace and follow.

Just before she fell asleep Fabia felt she could see a long line of Minsters coming down the centuries from the first one, who had built Queen's Hoo, until they reached the Duke.

And he was not the end, but the beginning of another series of generations. Their children and their children's children would all find at Queen's Hoo the help, the love, and the vibrations which had been waiting for him at the moment when he most needed them.

"I will not fail him," Fabia vowed to herself as she fell asleep, "and neither will he fail the future!"

Chapter Seven

Fabia awoke with a feeling of such intense happiness that she could not bear to open her eyes and leave the dream-world in which she was in the Duke's arms and his lips were on hers.

"I love you! I love you!"

She said it in her mind over and over again until gradually reality asserted itself and she realised she was alone and that the sunshine was flooding in through the windows, from which the curtains had been drawn back.

'It must be very late,' she thought.

She looked across the room to see that the communicating-door into the Sitting-Room was open and she knew that was where Hannah would be waiting for her to wake.

But she did not wish to speak to Hannah or anybody else. She wanted just to savour her own happiness, which she felt was like a fountain springing into the sky where the Duke had carried her last night and she had known that they both touched the Divine.

It was hard to believe now that when she had come from the garden upstairs to bed she had been so unhappy that her whole world had fallen in pieces and she was left only with an agony that was physical as well as mental.

Now everything was transformed and she knew it was Queen's Hoo which had brought her and the Duke together.

If she had not been here when he arrived, they might have gone through life without each other, both handicapped because alone they could never have been complete.

Then, because she suddenly felt an urgency to be with the Duke and to make sure he had not forgotten her since she had left him, she sat up in bed.

As if she sensed her wakefulness, Hannah came into the room.

"Well, you've certainly had a good sleep!" she said in her calm, matter-of-fact manner.

"It was something I did not do until after dawn."

"Now, it's no use worrying yourself..." Hannah began, but Fabia interrupted her.

"I am not worrying," she said, "I am happy! So marvellously, rapturously happy that I cannot believe it is real!"

Hannah looked at her in surprise. Then she asked quickly:

"What's happened? Why are you speaking like that?"

"I can hardly believe it," Fabia replied, "But I am to marry the Duke, and I know it would please Mama, because he loves me as I love him!"

For a moment Hannah stared at her incredulously, then she asked in a strange voice:

"Is this true?"

"Yes, it is really true," Fabia replied, "and we are to be married here very quietly in the Church in the Park."

"God be thanked!" Hannah exclaimed. "My prayers have been answered!"

Her voice broke and the tears ran down her cheeks, but as Fabia held her hands out to her she turned away, as if ashamed of her weakness, and said:

"The sooner you get up the better! I expect His Grace will be wanting to see you."

* * *

The Duke had also slept late, and when he woke he wondered if his Valet would be worried as to what had happened to him.

Like Fabia, he wished not to hurry but to lie thinking of his happiness and how he had found unexpectedly what he had always been seeking although at the time he had not been aware of it.

Now he knew why every other woman to whom he had made love had disappointed him, why he had grown so quickly bored, and why he had done a great many outrageous things simply to relieve the monotony of going from one love-affair to another.

"This is different," he told himself, "so very, very different, and I shall never be bored again."

At the same time, he could not help wondering what he could do to live up to Fabia's ideals and her belief that he must help and influence other people in a way quite different from anything he had ever done before.

The Duke was aware that there were in fact a few improvements he could make on his Estates and concerning the welfare of his tenants and employees. But he was not anxious to make his mark, as Fabia had suggested, in the House of Lords.

There were plenty of politicians dedicated to their work there, and he knew he found his fellow Peers on the whole rather a dull lot and he had no particular desire to associate with them.

"I wonder what I can do?" he asked, and felt it was a question that he must put not only to himself but to his grandmother and Queen's Hoo.

With a slight smile he thought they had now taken a hand in running his affairs, so it was up to them to carry on, as they doubtless intended to do anyway.

When finally he got out of bed, he went to his own room to find as he expected that his Valet was waiting for him with a worried expression on his face.

"I wondered what had happened to Your Grace,"

he said. "I thought at first Your Grace must have gone riding. But then I saw your clothes were still here."

"I chose to sleep in the Duchess's room last night," the Duke answered.

As he spoke he saw the Valet glance at his tumbled bed and knew the man was well aware why he had done so.

As if in answer to his unspoken question the Valet said:

"Major Bicester was asking for Your Grace a short while ago, and when I tells him Your Grace was not to be found, he left for London and asked me to say that he'd be back in two days' time."

Accepting this information without comment, the Duke went into the adjoining room to have his bath.

As he washed, he thought everything had worked out perfectly.

Because he had been so tired he had slept on, thus avoiding the embarrassment of having to decide whether or not he should say good-bye to Gigi, with the likelihood of her complaining because he was sending her away.

Now that they were gone and he was alone with Fabia, the first thing to do was to plan their marriage.

By the time he was dressed the Duke had decided that he would go at once to see the Vicar of the Church and arrange the date.

As both he and Fabia were residents in the Parish there would be no need for a Special Licence, and when Eddie returned he could be his Best Man, with Hannah perhaps the only other witness at the Ceremony.

The Duke felt his heart quicken at the thought that then Fabia would be his wife!

His love for her would be very different from anything he had ever felt before, and the rapture of being her husband and teaching her about love would open new horizons.

He felt he was almost like a School-boy contemplating

the holidays with the joy and excitement of anticipation which were often more vivid than the realisation.

But the Duke was sure there would be no disappointments when Fabia was his wife.

She was everything he needed in a woman, and because of her sensitivity she would be exactly the right sort of Duchess that the family and tradition required.

"She loves me as a man," he told himself, and knew that was irrefutably true.

* * *

The Duke came back from the Vicarage eager to tell Fabia what he had arranged, and he found that she had learnt where he had gone and was standing outside the house waiting for him.

He had driven in his Phaeton to see the Vicar because he knew that he and Fabia would want to ride together later in the day. He also thought he should make his visit a formal one.

He found that the Vicar was an old man whom he remembered well and who had been a friend and protégé of his grandmother.

He was delighted to see the Duke and honoured that he should have the privilege of solemnising his wedding.

"I have often thought of Your Grace," he said in his quiet, scholarly voice, "and hoped that I should see you again at Queen's Hoo before I died."

"From now on you will see me here a great deal," the Duke answered, "because although as you know I have other houses, this is the one that both my future wife and I will always love the best."

He knew his answer delighted the Vicar, and when he asked him to keep the intended marriage secret, the Duke knew that there would be no question of anybody being aware of what was taking place until it was over.

He arranged the time, and when the Vicar saw him to the door he said:

"I have know Fabia since she was a little girl. She

is a very exceptional person and in my opinion a young woman with a personality and character which are rare."

He paused for a moment before he went on:

"I know Your Grace will not think it an impertinence when I say that when I am with her I find her in many ways a younger edition of our beloved Duchess."

"That is what I thought myself," the Duke replied.

When he drove back to the house and saw Fabia waiting for him, he thought there was a rightness about her, as if the house was a frame for her and she belonged there as much as he did himself.

She ran towards him as he stepped down from the Phaeton, and instead of going into the house they walked into the garden.

For a moment there was no need to talk and they both were content just to be together.

Only when they reached the Water Garden did the Duke say:

"You are even lovelier today than you were last night in the moonlight."

"D-did it . . . really happen?" Fabia asked. "And did you say you . . . loved me?"

They were out of sight of the house, shielded by the rhododendron bushes brilliant with crimson and white blossoms. Slowly, as if he savoured the moment, the Duke put his arms round Fabia.

"I loved you last night," he said. "This morning I love you much more and you are more beautiful than I remembered when I awoke."

Fabia gave a little laugh of sheer happiness.

Then he was kissing her and it was impossible for them to think of anything but each other for a long time.

At last she asked:

"Where have you been? Or shall I guess?"

"I think you know."

"Barker told me you had gone to the village, and I thought in fact it might be to the Vicarage."

"You were quite right," the Duke said, "and it is all arranged. We will be married three days from now. I am only waiting so long for two reasons."

Fabia looked at him enquiringly.

"One, I am waiting for Eddie to return and be my Best Man, and secondly, my darling, your wedding-gown cannot be here until then."

"My . . . wedding-gown?"

The Duke smiled.

"I have sent a groom to London to order a number of gowns which you will need for your trousseau, but first and most urgent is the gown in which you are to be married."

Fabia drew in her breath.

"How can you think of . . . anything so . . . wonderful? I know that clothes are unimportant beside what we . . . feel for each other but I did not . . . wish you to be ashamed of . . . me."

The Duke drew her closer to him.

"I will never be that," he answered, "but I am also well aware how important gowns are to a woman, especially on the most important day of her life."

"How could it be anything else . . . when I am marrying you?" Fabia asked. "But are you sure it will fit me?"

"I made certain of that. My Valet obtained your measurements from Hannah, but I said she was not to tell you because I wanted to do so myself."

"How could any man be . . . so thoughtful . . . . so understanding?" Fabia asked.

"You will not have to teach me to think about you," the Duke said. "In the past I have often been told I am selfish, but where you are concerned I promise I will think about you first and myself a very long way behind."

"I shall think of you . . . and only you."

The Duke kissed her.

Then as if they remembered where they were going they walked on towards the Temple.

They sat down on the steps and looked out on the exquisite vista in front of them, which each time seemed to the Duke more beautiful than it had ever been before.

Then without speaking he put his arms round Fabia and kissed her until he knew that her heart was beating as quickly as his and they were both a little breathless.

"Now tell me," he said in a voice that was unsteady, "that my vibrations are what you want them to be and as they were when I was young."

"They are so . . . strong now that they are almost . . . overpowering," Fabia answered, "and now that the barriers which stopped their flow are down, they are vivid, intense, and irresistible."

"As long as to you they are irresistible that is all that matters," the Duke went on, but Fabia knew there was a note of triumph in his voice.

When a long time later they walked back arm-in-arm towards the house, she felt it was not just imagination but he really had a new air of determination and authority about him.

It was as if love had given him a new purpose in life.

She looked up at him adoringly and he thought the expression in her eyes was so lovely and so poignant that no artist, however talented, could ever capture it on canvass.

Nevertheless, he said:

"The first thing I will arrange after our honeymoon is over is to have you painted the way you look now. I will hang the picture on the wall of my Study, and carry it with me wherever I go, so that you will always be there to guide and inspire me, and I shall know even if you are not with me what you want me to do."

"I want to be with you," Fabia said.

"You will be," the Duke replied, "and that, my darling, is something of which you can be very sure."

They walked in through the garden-door and as

they went along the passage which led to the Hall, Barker came hurrying towards them, saying:

"I've been looking for Your Grace."

"What is it?" the Duke enquired.

"A gentleman from London wishes to see Your Grace!"

The Duke frowned.

"From London?"

"Yes, Your Grace. His name is Mr. John Colliston, and he has called on behalf of Lord Stanley."

The Duke looked puzzled.

"Lord Stanley?" he repeated almost beneath his breath.

Fabia looked at him questioningly.

"What is it?" she asked. "What does this gentleman want with you?"

"I have no idea," the Duke replied. "But Lord Stanley, whom I know quite well, is the Secretary of State for War and the Colonies."

Fabia's eyes widened, and as they followed Barker towards the Hall she walked beside the Duke in silence. She wondered if she should leave him, but his arm was still linked with hers.

Barker opened the door of the Morning-Room and they saw standing at the window looking out onto the sunlit garden a tall man holding a despatch-case in his hand.

As they entered he turned and walked eagerly towards the Duke, holding out his hand.

"Good-morning, Your Grace," he said. "Forgive me for calling without an appointment, but the matter is urgent, and Lord Stanley asked me to come here with all possible speed."

"I am only surprised," the Duke said, "that you were able to find me. I thought nobody knew my whereabouts."

Mr. Colliston smiled.

"It was very difficult to extract Your Grace's address from your Secretary at Minster House, and it was in fact only when I informed him that it was on Her Majesty's orders that I was trying to find you that he told me where you were."

"Her Majesty?"

Fabia realised that the Duke had stiffened, and she said in a low voice:

"Perhaps you would like me to leave you?"

"No, of course not," the Duke said firmly. "Let me introduce you to Mr. John Colliston. Miss Fabia Wilton is a relative of mine."

Mr. Colliston bowed and there was no mistaking the look of admiration in his eyes when Fabia, having dropped him a curtsey, held out her hand.

"Suppose we sit down?" the Duke suggested. "I cannot possibly imagine what you have to say that has brought you here so precipitately."

There was a touch of sarcasm in his voice and Fabia thought he was anticipating that Mr. Colliston was bringing him bad news and was somehow preparing himself to hear it.

Mr. Colliston put his despatch-case on his knees and unlocked it with a small gold key attached to his watch-chain.

"I have it here in writing, Your Grace," he said, "in a letter from Lord Stanley, but perhaps you would rather I told you what His Lordship says in simple words."

"I think that might be easier," the Duke replied.

Fabia glanced at him and thought there was a wary look in his eyes and she knew too that he was tense.

It seemed too unkind that something should spoil their happiness at this particular moment, and she prayed fervently that what Mr. Colliston had to impart would not be something unpleasant or disturbing.

"Briefly, Your Grace," Mr. Colliston said, as he took some papers from his despatch-case, "Lord Stanley, with the full approval of Her Majesty the Queen, wishes to offer you the post of Governor-General of India!"

There was an astonished silence. Then as if he felt he could not have heard aright, the Duke asked:

"Did you say—Governor-General of India?"

"Yes, Your Grace. The Earl of Auckland's term of office ends in September, and Lord Stanley could think of nobody better fitted to take his place than yourself."

"And you say this idea has the approval of Her Majesty?"

"Her Majesty chose your name first, Your Grace, from those Lord Stanley presented for her approval."

The Duke thought a little cynically that while Her Majesty might think him a good choice for the post in question, to send him to India would also keep him out of mischief and prevent him from involving her Ladies-in-Waiting in scandal.

Then as he hesitated, thinking that to leave England for a number of years was a step he had never contemplated and for the moment he was unable to envisage what that would entail, he felt Fabia's hand slip into his.

He then knew without words that this was what she had visualised for him when she had spoken of him as a Ruler, and it was in fact not only a position of great authority but one in which he could influence and inspire the millions of people under his control.

"I do not need to tell Your Grace," Mr. Colliston was saying, "that there is no position in the world today of such authority and at the same time of such great responsibility as that of Governor-General in India."

He gave a little laugh as he said:

"You will rule over a country almost as large as Europe, and I know that many of your ancestors, especially your grandfather, contributed to the history of the British in India."

"I remember that too," the Duke said with a smile.

"As a matter of fact," Mr. Colliston went on, "the Marquis, as he was then, was one of my heroes when I was at School, and it broke my heart when I was not strong enough to join the Army and was forced instead to go to the Foreign Office."

"I have heard Lord Stanley speak highly of you," the Duke said, "and you have made a success of your second choice."

"And you will soon emulate the achievements of your grandfather," Mr. Colliston said with a boyish enthusiasm.

He put the papers he had taken from his case on the chair beside him.

"These will tell Your Grace all you need to know about your duties as Governor-General," he said. "I expect you are aware that the Earl of Auckland has involved India in an utterly disastrous Afghan war, the effects of which Your Grace will be expected to minimise."

"I have not yet said I will accept the position," the Duke expostulated.

As he spoke he felt Fabia's fingers tighten on his and knew she had already decided what his answer would be and there was no question of his refusing.

He looked down at her with a smile. Then he said:

"I know it will make no difference to Her Majesty's decision. It will indeed enhance my qualifications, but I shall in fact be taking my wife with me to India."

"Your wife?" Mr. Colliston exclaimed. "That is indeed good news, Your Grace. Lord Stanley was saying only yesterday that he hoped you would marry, because a Governor-General always finds a wife indispensable in dealing with the Maharajahs and other Princes whose own wives, of course, are in Purdah."

"I am sure my wife will do everything that is expected of her," the Duke said.

As he spoke he felt as if Fabia's fingers quivered in his and was aware how pleased she was.

Because he felt her excitement transmit itself to him, he said:

"I think, Mr. Colliston, you should join us in celebrating both our engagement and my new post."

"I will certainly drink to your health, Your Grace, and I also congratulate you most warmly and wish you and Miss Wilton every happiness in the future!"

"You are the first to do so," the Duke said, "but may I ask you to keep it a secret, except of course from Lord Stanley?"

"You can trust me, Your Grace."

The Duke rang a bell and ordered a bottle of champagne.

When it came, Mr. Colliston raised his glass to toast them before he said solemnly:

"I would like to say, Your Grace, that your appointment will be received with great pleasure, not only by everybody in the Government and your many admirers in the field of sport, but also by all those who work in India. They will believe, as I do, that you are exactly the right person needed at the moment in that strange and beautiful but often turbulent land."

He spoke with such sincerity that Fabia thought it was very moving, and as Mr. Colliston raised his glass to his lips she lifted hers too in a silent salute to the man she loved.

After Mr. Colliston had left, saying he had to get back to London with all possible speed to carry the good news to Lord Stanley, the Duke said:

"I can hardly believe it is true! I never in my wildest dreams imagined myself as Governor-General of India."

"Papa was in India for two years and he told me so much about it," Fabia said, "I might have known it was the place you were most needed and where all your organising ability and leadership would be shown to its best."

"I believe there are a great many problems in the country, but apart from the Earl of Auckland there have been many admirable Governors."

"As you will be," Fabia said softly. "and the difficulties are there only for you to smoothe them out or obliterate them."

"How could I fail to be successful when you are beside me?" the Duke asked.

He looked at her. Then he held out his arms.

She ran into them and he held her very close to him but for the moment he did not kiss her.

"You have won again, my precious," he said, "and I have the feeling that perhaps it was your vibrations which made first Lord Stanley and then the Queen choose me for this particular post."

"I hope so," Fabia said, "but I think in fact it was because, as Mr. Colliston said, there was nobody better fitted for the position than you."

"There will be a great deal that must be done," the Duke said quietly, "but we will do it together, and when you are beside me I feel I can rule not only India but the whole Universe!"

He was joking and yet there was a note of seriousness in his words.

Fabia turned her face up to his and put her arm round his neck to pull his head down towards hers.

"I love you," she whispered, "and my love will help you and protect you whatever you are doing."

"That is all I ask," the Duke answered, "and because our love for each other is greater than anything in the world, there will be no barriers, no restrictions and no limits to what we can achieve together, my precious!"

Then he was kissing her, kissing her fiercely, demandingly, with an insistence that told Fabia he needed her love in a way that was different.

He was not only wooing her, he was conquering her, and while he was prepared for her to help and guide him, he also wanted her to surrender herself to his dominance because he was a man and she was his woman.

She understood what he was feeling, and she was aware that just as the years of idleness were past, so was his resistance to everything which he did not wish to understand or which was spiritually greater than himself.

Now he was prepared to accept the vibrations in which she believed and to realise that they gave him a new power, a new strength, and a new ability to rule.

The Duke raised his head.

"I love you!" he said. "God, how I love you, and my darling, you are mine—mine completely, now and for eternity!"

She knew as she spoke that his vibrations, strong, vibrant, and compelling, reached out towards her, and she was held captive by them and there was no escape.

"I am . . . yours!" she murmured against the Duke's lips.

Then he was kissing her again, kissing her until he was carrying her up towards the stars and nothing had any importance except their love.

ABOUT THE AUTHOR

BARBARA CARTLAND, the world's most famous romantic novelist, who is also an historian, playwright, lecturer, political speaker and television personality, has now written over 300 books.

She has also had many historical works published and has written hour autobiographies as well as the biographies of her mother and that of her brother Ronald Cartland, who was the first Member of Parliament to be killed in W.W. II. This book has a preface by Sir Winston Churchill and has just been republished with an introduction by Sir Arthur Bryant.

Barbara Cartland has sold 200 million books over the world, more than half of these in the U.S.A. She broke the world record in 1975 by writing twenty-three books and the four subsequent years with 20, 21, 23 and 24. In addition her album of love songs has just been published, sung with the Royal Philharmonic Orchestra.

Barbara Cartland, who is a Dame of the Order of St. John of Jerusalem, has championed the cause for old people and founded the first Romany Gypsy Camp in the world.

Barbara Cartland is deeply interested in vitamin therapy and is President of the British National Association for Health. Her book, *The Magic of Honey*, has sold millions all over the world.

She has a magazine, *The World of Romance*, and her Barbara Cartland Romantic World Tours will, in conjunction with British Airways, carry travelers to England, Egypt, India, France, Germany and Turkey.

Barbara Cartland

The world's bestselling author of romantic fiction. Her stories are always captivating tales of intrigue, adventure and love.

☐ 20234	SHAFT OF SUNLIGHT	$1.95
☐ 20014	GIFT OF THE GODS	$1.95
☐ 20126	AN INNOCENT IN RUSSIA	$1.95
☐ 20013	RIVER OF LOVE	$1.95
☐ 14503	THE LIONESS AND THE LILY	$1.75
☐ 13942	LUCIFER AND THE ANGEL	$1.75
☐ 14084	OLA AND THE SEA WOLF	$1.75
☐ 14133	THE PRUDE AND THE PRODIGAL	$1.75
☐ 13032	PRIDE AND THE POOR PRINCESS	$1.75
☐ 13984	LOVE FOR SALE	$1.75
☐ 14248	THE GODDESS AND THE GAIETY GIRL	$1.75
☐ 14360	SIGNPOST TO LOVE	$1.75
☐ 14361	FROM HELL TO HEAVEN	$1.75
☐ 13985	LOST LAUGHTER	$1.75
☐ 14750	DREAMS DO COME TRUE	$1.95
☐ 14902	WINGED MAGIC	$1.95
☐ 14922	A PORTRAIT OF LOVE	$1.95

Buy them at your local bookstore or use this handy coupon for ordering:

Bantam Books, Inc., Dept. BC2, 414 East Golf Road, Des Plaines, Ill. 60016

Please send me the books I have checked above. I am enclosing $_____ (please add $1.00 to cover postage and handling). Send check or money order —no cash or C.O.D.'s please.

Mr/Mrs/Miss_____

Address_____

City_____State/Zip_____

BC2—2/82

Please allow four to six weeks for delivery. This offer expires 8/82.